I0768106

In Trust We Fall

A Collection of Short Stories

By Tabatha Shipley

Tabatha Shipley

Also by Tabatha Shipley

Kingdom of Fraun Novels

Breaking Eselda

Redeeming Jordyn

Training Tutor

Empowering Sawchett

Tin's Tale and other stories of Fraun

Kingdom of Fraun (omnibus)

Stand Alone Novels

30 Days Without Wings

Projection

A Spark of Magic

Noises from the Other Side

How to Schedule a Death

Table of Contents

Scintillate

This story was born in the idea journal as so many of my great ones are. Loosely inspired by the decor at a beautiful restaurant my husband and I went to for an anniversary celebration, this one really came to life once I let my overactive imagination free. It would be an interesting parlor trick and something that would certainly keep restaurants full. So, enjoy the story, and ask yourself: would you trust this booth?

My job is to point people toward true love. No, I'm not Cupid. I don't fly. In fact, I don't move at all.

I am the corner booth at Scintillate, the most upscale and expensive restaurant in old town Scottsdale, Arizona. I hear people talk about their experiences outside the walls of my restaurant and it sounds like a nice neighborhood. Fancy restaurants are on every corner and you have to wait a long time to get even the lowliest of seats.

Imagine how long you have to wait for me.

My plush red seating is wiped down after every customer but steamed every night. The floors under my table, raised a step higher than those of the rest of the restaurant, are swept and polished regularly. Even the table that shares the space with me, oblivious as he may be, is a gorgeous, dark, gleaming specimen.

I'm sure there are a hundred, possibly even a thousand, booths just like me in the world. We are in the far corners of restaurants, secluded and quiet. Our lighting is absolutely perfect. We are in the spot most likely to be seen by waitstaff, meaning your drinks will never be left empty and waiting for more.

But what makes me special is that I was gifted with the ability to see love. It's not a line. It's the truth. On the day I was stitched together, my maker cast a spell. She gifted me the chance to see the path of a couple's future, based on one dinner. I could see the options before them. I could tell them what love holds for them. I could tell them about their true love.

Once couples heard about me, you can imagine the reaction. Each night I tick through two or three couples on my waiting list. I read their innermost thoughts. I read their futures. Then, when they are ready to pay their bill and depart, I give them the wisdom.

Whether they like it or not.

February 25-Couple #1

It's eleven days past the holiday known as Valentine's Day. I'm pretty sure I'm still dealing with customers who attempted to book a seat with me for the auspicious evening. That was a busy night; we squeezed in four customers before closing. Tonight, as the doors are opened and the kitchen fires up, Jorge comes to me. He's my favorite host right now. He believes I can understand him, which I can. Some of the other employees make fun of him for it, but he talks to me anyway.

"Two couples," he tells me in a voice barely above a whisper. "The first one is a married couple who sounded a little more seasoned."

This is his way of telling me they sound like they've been together for a while. They're not newlyweds or a young couple. Of course, most of my clients aren't. The prices on this menu aren't exactly conducive to tight budgets.

Jorge swipes a rag over my already clean table, possibly a ruse to cover the fact that he's talking to me again. "I'll be right here with you, making sure they understand the policy. Good luck."

He's gone before the last word has faded into the night, back toward his area where he will greet customers and show only the select pairs we've discussed back to me for our evening of exploration.

I can hardly wait.

They slide into my booth unevenly. She takes an almost dainty seat, careful to perch lightly on the material as if she may hurt me. She won't, but I appreciate the gesture. He, on the other hand, plops into the seat as if testing my springs.

"Mr. and Mrs. Winslow," Jorge begins, "welcome to Scintillate." He hands a menu to each of them.

Mr. Winslow opens it immediately, letting out a low whistle. "This food better be good," he says. "Did you see these prices?"

"It's a celebration," his wife says. "How often do we do this?"

There's a short pause. Then, when it becomes evident Mr. Winslow doesn't intend to answer, Jorge continues. "I need to explain a few things to you, briefly, before you begin your meal tonight. The booth you are seated in is magic. During your meal, the booth can scan your innermost thoughts and, some people believe, your true heart. At the end of the evening, the booth will render a reading for you about your future as it pertains specifically to your love life. Do you both understand and consent to the reading of the booth? I must remind you that, should you choose to consent, there is nothing any of us can do to influence the booth to give a reading that we would like. In that same vein, nothing you get from the booth will be a guarantee. That is to say that you can use that information in any way that you see fit. Including, some have said, taking the information as a warning and attempting to change that future you are shown."

"We get it—" Mr. Winslow cuts off. "We're hungry. Can we order with you or are we waiting for someone else?"

His impatience seems rude. But I can tell what it really is. Mr. Winslow is nervous. He is afraid that I will see what he fears. He is afraid that I will read him accurately and tell him things he doesn't want to hear.

"No problem, sir. Just, for prosperity's sake, can you agree to the terms I've outlined?"

"We agree," Mrs. Winslow says. There is no trace of hesitancy or worry in her voice. She sounds perfectly composed and confident.

"Wonderful, let me get your server. Have a lovely meal." Jorge's steps fade away and from that point on, I focus on the couple seated with me at the booth.

I didn't like his attitude from the start, so I decide to begin with Mr. Winslow.

The first thing you should know about my gift is that you can learn a lot about a person by scanning their memories. There are a lot of things locked in your unconscious mind that clue people into what your future may have in store. If, for example, you spent your childhood being bullied and teased for never being good enough for girls to find attractive, like our Mr. Winslow here, you may never be able to shake the feeling that there's some truth to that.

I scan the memories of years and years and years in a matter of minutes. Mr. Winslow has barely sipped his first glass of wine and sampled his appetizer before I can already feel that pain deeply in my cushions. Teasing by older boys, taunting by older girls, and ruined relationships because he was convinced that he was never going to be good enough. This man doubts that his wife truly loves him. Deep down, he believes that she is waiting for the right moment to leave him. He wonders how much of their marriage has been faked because she couldn't find someone better.

I snap myself to the present moment before his deep sadness can drag me down further. The hardest part about my job is that I have nothing to relate these readings to. I don't get to live a life outside of these walls. I've never had relationships at all, certainly none like this. So when I scan someone, I adopt all of their experiences. When they're hard ones, like this, I can feel that pain but I can't always explain it. The conversation floats around me for a bit, bringing me back to the present.

"This is delicious," Mrs. Winslow coos.

"It's good," Mr. Winslow agrees. "I don't know if it was worth all this wait and money, honestly." His voice drops a little lower. "Is there something you wanted to tell me? Maybe you're hoping that this booth—" he bounces a bit as if to indicate me— "will tell me for you?" I know what he's asking. I know what he fears. I'm almost afraid to scan for the answer on his behalf.

But that's my job so I dive into the scan of his wife's past.

There's pain here too. One thing I've learned about people is that there is pain in all of you. No one escapes these daily experiences without some kind of fear, anger, or hurt. I cannot ever find a future for any of you that completely removes it, either. Some people have more than their fair share, sure. In fact, what some customers believe is their worst pain wouldn't even register as uncomfortable for others. But it is still painful for them. It always amazes me how different you can all be, and yet you share the same basic emotions. Sometimes I wish I could experience emotions for myself, instead of through all of you.

Mrs. Winslow doesn't have anything deep like the trauma of bullying that her husband has. An extreme sort of loneliness threads through her entire childhood instead. There's this sense of isolation, of being invisible. Then, as if someone flipped on the bright cleaning lights in her dark restaurant, there's someone who sees her.

The memories of this boy are clear. She calls him Andrew and she likes him right away. I sense the way she leans toward him, the way he makes her feel like she belongs. He makes her feel seen.

When I pull back to the present, I'm warm and content. I have a new understanding of how this couple balances now based on their past. He never believed he deserved a girl but this girl needed someone to see her. He was that boy. I wish I could tell him that what she feels is real because he needs to hear it.

But there is more for me to do.

As the main course is dropped in front of the couple, I begin to read their futures.

The second thing you should know is that futures are never certain. It's not unlike the way my stitching was done by my creator. I will look for a pattern that includes both of these two individuals. I will analyze how they weave and cross. There will be many options to choose from. I will have to pick one and weave the most likely future from what threads I'm given. It can be difficult because often those threads that include both parties are small. Oftentimes the true love component of my talent means two people cannot be part of the same tapestry. There is no way for me to force them together for a future, at least not one without pain.

I imagine the threads in my mind for the Winslows. I pull at the thread for him, the boy she called Andrew. Then I pull at the one for her. I'm pleased to see many possibilities include both of them. Perhaps, despite the harsh way he presented himself, they are truly meant to be together. I pull at a few possibilities as they eat their dinner, pleasantly chatting about the menu and the weather. Their bottle of wine is finished and they discuss dessert options. By the time they've finished, the picture I've created is lovely indeed.

I push the information out to a device somewhere near Jorge. I know he will retrieve the paper and bring it to the couple with their bill. I hope they'll be satisfied when they read it. It's not every day that I get to bring a happy future to a couple.

There is a future for the two of you in which you have an adorable home in a small town. I see you sitting on the porch in chairs, side by side, happily talking about your day. I see the way you look at each other. More importantly, I feel the way you make each other feel. There is a comfort each of you finds with one another. There is a happiness there that I don't often feel between two people. It is as though you are made for each other and belong together. Congratulations on finding a future that seems so bright. All of the paths I see look long and prosperous.

"This is beautiful," Mrs. Winslow says. Her voice breaks a little and I feel her happiness.

Mr. Winslow leans in and plants a kiss on her cheek. I feel the surprise from him. He was expecting something else entirely. He was expecting me to tell him she belonged with someone else. He was expecting me to break his heart. He feels different now, more confident. I have given him that, and I'm proud of myself for it.

Jorge's footsteps return. "Alright, you are all set. I hope you had a nice experience. Here's your card back. Have a great night."

Once they both stand beside the table, I can no longer scan or read them. I can still hear them as he helps her with her coat. Both of them, I notice, sound more light and free than they did before they arrived. Again, I'm proud of myself for being able to give them that.

"Michael, I'm so glad we did this."

It's her voice. But I'm confused by the sentence. Did she call him Michael?

It's hard to remember, with the connection broken. The memories are fading. Didn't she always call him Andrew? Wasn't the boy in the memories—the one who saw her—wasn't he Andrew? Didn't my vision relate to a man named Andrew?

Try as I might, I cannot recall any memories of

Mr. Winslow's that used his name. Why had I assumed Andrew was Mr. Winslow? With the connection broken, I cannot remember enough detail to know.

The memories begin to fade as the happy couple, now confident in their future, walk out into the night. I imagine them holding hands, smiling at each other.

I wonder if I have just fixed a doomed marriage or if I have made a terrible mistake.

February 25-Couple #2

Jorge is back, wiping a rag over the table that has already been cleaned. "This next couple is younger, starry-eyed. Good luck."

He's not gone for long before he's back, leading two women. They drop onto my seat and I immediately feel a sense of enjoyment radiating from both, as if they are sharing some kind of private joke. It's a calming feeling.

"Ladies, welcome to Scintillate." Jorge hands a menu to each of them, just as he does with every couple. "I need to explain a few things to you before you begin your meal tonight." He continues through his entire prepared speech, this time uninterrupted by the couple.

I don't feel any hesitancy from these two. I do feel skepticism underneath that sense of humor they seem to share. They don't believe in the magic, but they're hoping to have a good time. "Do you both agree to the terms I've outlined?" Jorge asks.

The woman on the right leans forward, putting her weight on the table. "Let me ask you something," she starts. Her voice is quiet, like a secret. "Do you really believe in all this?" she asks. "This is really a magic booth?"

"After the things I have heard come out of this booth, I cannot believe anything but the truth. This booth truly is magic," Jorge says. "But, again, what you do with the information that comes to you tonight is completely up to you."

"What do we have to lose, Steph?" the other young woman asks. "It'll be fun."

"I'm marrying you no matter what this cushion says," Steph answers.

"Good." The two women share a laugh.

Jorge repeats the line the restaurant requires him to say. "So you agree to the terms?"

"Oh, yes. Of course," the woman who is not Steph agrees. "We're all set."

"Yes. Read our future, Mr. Booth," Steph says. She runs her hands over the cushion. If I could laugh, I would laugh with them. I like the spirit running through these two. There's something light and fun about the experience I'm sharing with them. It's intoxicating.

"Wonderful, let me get your server. Have a lovely meal." Jorge's steps fade away and I get to work.

Their pasts are unremarkable. The one called Angela in her memories grew up in a loving family. She went to college, met a boy, got married, and had a son. But then things fell apart. There was a lot of isolation from those memories. I feel Angela's loneliness, her confusion, her pain.

Steph grew up in a family with a lot of

children. There was a sense of not standing out, of being unremarkable. She went to college and then made a career for herself. The feeling that this is the way she will make herself stand out is running through everything. Steph has something to prove to the world.

In both of their memories, the moment they met is a shade of confusion. At first, I don't understand. But the reactions of other people to their relationship starts to clue me in. Apparently, neither of them had ever been with someone of the same gender before. They weren't sure how it would be received. There are some bad experiences there, for sure. But they're not all bad.

It's the futures that cause me to slow down. Sometimes, when I read a couple, there are no futures that involve both parties. That causes me a sense of almost sadness if that feeling were possible for me. I know it will cause them pain, temporarily, to hear about those futures. But I also know, because I get the benefit of seeing how the thread continues from that point, that it is for the best and they will both be alright in the end. This couple isn't like that. This couple has so many threads that involve both of them, that it's hard for me to see past what is already forming a solid tapestry before my eyes.

Some paths lead to anger, pain, and yelling. I don't like those, but I have to watch a few of them to be sure. They want different things when I follow these paths. The thing is, underneath their pain and anger I can tell they both want the other to be happy. They both want what is truly best for the other partner. It's unselfish, it's raw. They're both willing to fight for the other person's chance to get what they want and need.

There are paths that lead to sadness, loneliness, and grief. One such path shows me a death that neither woman is truly ready for. There's an accident down that path, one that both women blame themselves for. It's hard to recover from that.

There are paths that show happiness, love, and joy. But honestly, they're few and far between.

So what do I report to this couple?

I follow many of the threads again as the women laugh their way through dessert, completely unaware of what sort of pain awaits them. I listen to arguments that may never happen. I watch crippling moments of pain and misery. I see fleeting moments of laughter in the chaos.

I know I'm running out of time to choose a message for the women. But I take the time to watch a few of the more painful options again.

This time, I notice something I probably should've noticed before. They're both in all of the possibilities. When Angela is crying, Steph is right there with her arm around her shoulder. When

Steph is angry about something, it's Angela who listens to the righteous anger. I scan quickly, confirming. Yes, always the two women. Happy, angry, sad … but together.

I push the information out to the device somewhere near Jorge. It's the best I can do. The smallest hope for what I see coming. I hope it's enough for them.

I wish I had good news to bring you because I can sense in your souls that you are good people. There are many challenges coming your way in the future. I cannot make it easier to know this truth, I cannot take it away. The challenges I see are not set in stone, but I see very few paths without something that will truly alter your lives. If there is any hope I can give you, it is this: throughout all the messiness and pain that may be awaiting you, I see you standing together to face it. I see futures in which you feel anger, but it is anger that you cannot give the other what she deserves, and not anger with each other. I see futures with sadness, but always with the support of your partner to guide you. Sometimes my gift is a burden because I cannot control the message I bring. I cannot promise you a future without pain. But, based on what I see, you have found the right person to navigate that future with. Good luck.

"Well …" It's Steph's voice that rings out first. I feel a little shock ripple through her. But then it fades. "It's better than I expected," she says.

"This is like poetry," Angela adds. "Did you read that line about navigating the future? That's beautiful." Her happiness feels genuine.

I wasn't expecting that. I think of the pain I've seen in their futures. The death that could await them. The accident I've watched three times, feeling it as though it were happening to someone I have met. Why are they happy? This future will hurt. This future will tear them down.

"You are satisfied?" Jorge asks, returning their payment envelope to them.

"We are," Steph answers. "Your booth has a way with words."

"I think he draws that from the guests," Jorge says. "He's pretty silent when there is no one here."

I think that was supposed to be a joke. No one laughs.

The connection falters as the women rise. The pain of the possible futures starts to fade. I listen to them chat with Jorge, thanking him for the amazing experience. I hear them compliment the chef. I wish those women the best.

As the futures fade, I realize the answer to the question I couldn't ask. Perhaps it's not about being promised a future without pain. Perhaps it's truly about finding the person who makes that pain bearable.

Jorge is back just a few beats later, holding a rag that smells like bleach. He wipes the surface of the table. Then he folds the rag in half and uses a clean section to start wiping down my back. "You did a good job tonight," he whispers as he works. "Two couples both left happy. I wasn't sure about that first couple. They came in so angry I had my doubts about how your reading would go. I'm impressed with you, as always."

I want to tell him I don't remember the first couple. The memories of the second couple are starting to fade as well. That is the blessing and the curse of this job.

Jorge sits down on the edge of the booth to reach across to the center. As soon as he makes contact, I flash on his past, which I've seen before. I choose to ignore most of what I see because Jorge is a friend and not someone who is paying me to read him. But tonight a future flashes through, demanding attention. I pull at the thread, just a little. I see an older Jorge with a teenager. They're in a kitchen, chopping up food and laughing. The feeling of satisfaction, of belonging, is so strong. It's the same feeling I get when Jorge whispers to me about the night. This is his family. This is his happiness.

He stands up, breaking the connection. Memories of what I just saw stay with me for a beat and then they start to fade. I realize I may have been tempted to send a report to him, had this connection gone on longer. Does Jorge even want to know his future? He's never asked, not in all our time together.

"Alright, I'll send Charles in to get you steamed after we're closed for the night. You rest up. Tomorrow you see three couples," Jorge tells me. "See you then." He pats my upholstery and turns back toward his host stand.

I focus on the quiet around me and on the lack of human connection. Without the emotions you're all plagued with, my existence is simple. Maybe someday I'll find a way to give you a little of the peace I feel at night. Until then, I'll continue to read your futures and bring you glimpses into where your true love lies.

The Boy in the Hall

The opening part of this story is inspired by real events, believe it or not. The rest of it was an exercise I undertook while drafting Noises From the Other Side and trying to get in touch with the "rules" of ghostly behavior for that world. Can you trust your eyes when it comes to apparitions like this?

I was twelve the first time I saw a ghost.

It was late, later than I should've been awake. I lay there waiting until the sounds filtering through the air vent, that comforting voice of the late-night news broadcaster, clicked off in my parents' room. Then I counted to 500.

You're probably thinking I fell asleep sometime during that count. That this was all some kind of dream that I thought was real. Right? Well, I can't think of any way to prove to you that I didn't fall asleep. But it doesn't change what came next and I was awake for that.

After I reached 500 the house had slipped into a sort of comfortable silence. Have you ever listened to a sleeping house late at night? It's not completely silent, not really. There are sounds like creaking and settling, sounds of people breathing or snoring. Plus the hum of appliances stored with energy just waiting to be given a task.

I listened to the quiet house until I was sure it was safe. Then I dug my battered copy of The Secret Garden and a flashlight out from under my pillow. Because that's what book nerds do when we're supposed to be sleeping. We read books. A task we'd be perfectly within our rights to do any time of day by any adult who is in charge. We convince ourselves that we're being rebels that way. This is how I know I was awake. I could feel the pages underneath my fingertips.

I read three pages before my flashlight beam winked out. I shook it. Then, when that failed to work, I banged it against my palms. The beam flickered, shining through my open door, into the hallway, and onto a boy. Then it flickered out.

My breath caught in my throat and I held it there, listening intently. Would I hear breathing? Footsteps? The unsheathing of a sword?

The silence grew and stretched.

As I let out a shaky exhale, I tried to convince myself that my eyes were playing tricks on me. It was crazy to think I'd seen anything. I told myself I was tired.

The silence lasted long enough that I started to believe it was my imagination. Afraid to leave the safety of a $9.88 specially priced blanket that would somehow protect me from evil and possibly swords, I unscrewed the top of the flashlight and dumped the batteries onto my legs. Working quickly, I blew on the batteries the same way we reactivate tired video game cartridges. Then I slid them back into the flashlight.

I locked my eyes on the darkness of the hallway where the figure had been moments before. I held my breath and turned the flashlight on.

In the shaking, weak beam he stood completely still. His dark brown hair fell in his eyes. He was wearing an ugly orange vest, an ironic sort of life vest you'd see on a weird fashion model. His hands were shoved deep in the front pockets of what seemed to be blue jeans. He was barefoot.

He didn't move. Neither did I. We just stared at each other until the beam winked out again.

Then I did what any other kid would do in my situation. I pulled my blanket over my head and tried to be as silent as possible. I whispered little prayers to a deity I wasn't sure I actually believed in. Prayed that I wouldn't hear anything. Prayed that I wouldn't see anything else. Definitely prayed that I wouldn't feel anything brush my leg.

I sat there like that for so long that I did fall asleep.

When I woke the next morning to full sunlight the memory seemed ridiculous. I let myself forget it ever happened.

Until it happened again.

***

Fast-forward a bit. I was thirteen for this next memory. I was sitting at the kitchen table with my parents, all the necessary ingredients to make burritos in front of us. I had a plate holding an empty tortilla waiting to be filled. My mother finished with the spoon for the spicy meat and handed it to me. I looked up at her and took in that she was not alone on that side of the table.

Instantly, I dropped my eyes back to the meat. "Everything alright?" Mom asked.

I gave her a weak smile because it was all I could manage. "Yeah, all good." This was the first time I had ever seen the ghost during the daytime. It's stupid, I know, but I was starting to think he only existed at night. Part of me thought maybe he was a figment of my tired mind. Maybe I did fall asleep before that first encounter and dreamt the entire thing. But I certainly wasn't asleep this time at the kitchen table during dinner.

I finished putting meat on my tortilla and risked another glance. He was there, in his stupid orange vest with his brown hair that looked somehow clean and prepared for a day he would never get to live. He was sitting in the chair next to my mother, the one that is always empty because there are only three of us who eat at this table. Can ghosts sit? That doesn't seem right. But he looked like he was sitting there. He had that same small smile he always wore playing at the corners of his mouth. It's like he was keeping a secret and he loved it. I wonder if it is the secret of him that I'm keeping.

Enough paying attention to him. I grabbed the spoon for the black beans and started piling things inside my tortilla. Neither of my parents was reacting to this extra body at the table. Dad had managed to overstuff his burrito and was attempting to wrap it. Mom had wrapped hers and had already taken her first bite.

It was almost unfair that this kid kept finding me. I had seen him a few times since that first night. Every time was the same: I stayed up too late, and I saw him by the beam of my flashlight. He was in the same clothes and standing in the hallway every time. Until that dinner, I had never seen him in the daytime, and certainly never at my kitchen table.

It became obvious that my hands were shaking when I managed to throw lettuce all over the tortilla instead of in the nice pile of things I had going. "Something on your mind?" Dad asked with a little chuckle in his voice. "Lettuce hear about it." He laughed at his stupid pun.

I rolled my eyes, which is the traditional response he expected when he was being ridiculous. Then I turned my attention to my burrito, rolling it carefully. I couldn't say it was my full attention because that would be a lie. Some of my attention was still on the orange vest kid. I don't know what I was expecting, but I didn't want to look away in case I missed it. Was he planning on talking, helping himself to a burrito, standing up and walking away, disappearing, pulling out a weapon? In that moment, all of those things felt completely, terrifyingly, possible.

I took a bite of my burrito, chewing slowly. When I brought my eyes back up from my plate, he was gone. No poof of smoke … just gone. Already, I was wondering if I imagined him. Already I was convincing myself that he was never really there.

***

Three weeks later, he found his way into yet another place in the house he had never been. I came home from school and stepped into my bedroom to drop my backpack on the floor of my closet. Then I headed into the kitchen and grabbed a snack. I came back, shutting my bedroom door with my foot, to sit down and get some work done.

There he was. Standing in the center of my room under my ceiling fan. His hands were shoved into his pockets but the smile was gone. Instead, he looked sort of sad. His eyes were downcast. I couldn't help it, I turned my head to see where he was looking.

My backpack was open.

"Did you do that?" I whispered. There was no response. He just stood there in that exact position, head tilted toward my backpack and looking sad.

I was at war within myself. Do I look at the backpack and inspect it for changes? Or do I stay in the doorway and keep an eye on the ghost in my bedroom interacting with my stuff?

For a year I saw this ghost, which is why I felt almost calm about his presence. But sitting down at the kitchen table, standing in my bedroom, appearing in the daytime, and messing with my backpack were not part of the game I thought we were playing. He was changing the rules.

In the end, I chose the backpack. I dropped to the floor and pulled every single item out of the canvas. Nothing was out of place, nothing was missing, nothing was changed. It looked like he unzipped it and that's all.

By the time I stood up, he was gone. In his place was my sense of confusion. Did he unzip the backpack or did I? Maybe I just never zipped it after I was finished. I couldn't remember the actual act of zipping it after my last-period class.

Maybe that was because I never did. I convinced myself that this was what must have happened. After all, ghosts couldn't unzip backpacks.

***

To the best of my recollection, the next event was the same night as the backpack incident. I remember going to sleep at a normal time. In fact, I'd wager I was asleep before my parents' television clicked off. I hadn't been sleeping well, likely because I was always waking up to find a ghost or read a book. I was pretty tired.

I woke up in the middle of the night. One of those times when you're suddenly awake and you aren't really sure why.

I stayed still in my bed, letting my senses come alive. It was silent in my room, I remember that. Oddly silent. I didn't hear the noises of the house or the ticking of my clock. It was also very dark. Usually, the light from the street outside filtered in around my curtains. We lived in a city where it was never fully dark. But that night, I don't remember the light. Then the cold that slowly creeps out to your limbs from the center of your body when you're frightened set in. The one that makes the hair on your arms stand up and your breathing quicken. The one that makes that cold line of sweat break out on your neck. I laid there perfectly still, waiting for something to happen.

Then it did.

My name—spoken in two slow syllables, each one sounding like an exhale of breath. Quiet, close, and absolutely terrifying. "Sonya."

I swallowed a sudden lump in my throat and slammed my eyes closed. I hoped I was asleep. I prayed this was some sort of crazy dream. I wanted to wake up, open my eyes to my normal bedroom, and laugh about this. Silently, I promised whatever deity was listening that I wouldn't be mad, I would think it was funny. Just let me open my eyes and see my normal bedroom. I opened my eyes and things were exactly the same: the pitch black was all-encompassing and suffocating in the silence.

My shaky intake of breath filled my ears, the sound that usually meant I would be bursting into tears soon. That checked out with the burning in my throat. I didn't want to cry alone in my bed in that scary reality. I wanted to wake up. I needed to wake up.

I slowly moved my hand until it was resting against my leg. I took a bit of skin between my thumb and forefinger and pinched as hard as I could. It hurt.

That was a bad sign, wasn't it?

I froze when the voice spoke again, this time sounding a little further away. "Tomorrow." It sounded like it had more substance behind it, more like a whisper than just an expelling of air.

Then the light was back around the edge of the curtain, along with the ambient noise of the house. My clock was ticking. Compared with the darkness a moment ago, the room looked positively glowing. I could see the outline of everything I owned.

I could even see the kid in the orange vest standing under my fan in the center of my room, sadly looking down at my backpack where I left it at the bottom of my closet.

***

He was with me the moment I woke up the next morning. I wasn't even sure how I fell back to sleep after that but the next thing I knew, the alarm clock was blaring and he was still standing there. His smile was back, which made me feel a little better.

He stayed in the hallway while I went to the bathroom, showered, and dressed. But when I emerged from the door, steam wafting out with me, he was standing there like he had been waiting. He followed me into the kitchen and sat at the table while I ate breakfast. I was not sure what was different about that day, but he didn't want me to be alone.

I couldn't explain why he didn't freak me out. After the previous night, he probably should have. Instead, something about his presence felt comforting. I enjoyed knowing that he was with me.

I slid my backpack on, said goodbye to my parents, and when I stepped outside he came along. We walked side-by-side like two friends up the street. The school was less than a mile away. I'd walked to it countless times. Straight up our street, stick to the sidewalk at the major road, and use the crosswalk to get to the small street the school was on.

I hit the crosswalk button at the only major intersection I had to pass through and waited. The light turned red for the major street and my little walking symbol appeared. I stepped out onto the road. I was more than halfway across when I felt the zipper give on my backpack. Everything started shifting and collapsed onto the road behind me.

I checked my surroundings: the walk symbol

was still lit, and the light was still red. I bent down and grabbed everything as quickly as I could. A car horn honked and I looked up. All I remember at that moment was the orange vest kid giving me the same expression I had witnessed last night before I fell asleep. That sad look down. But he wasn't looking at the backpack, he was looking at me.

***

"Sonya, can you hear me?"

I open my eyes to see the intersection near the school. I'm on the sidewalk, which doesn't make sense because wasn't I just in the street? I blink a few times, trying to figure out what is wrong with my eyes. It doesn't seem as bright as it did before. It's like there's fog.

"Sonya?"

I turn my head toward the voice, not sure who it belongs to. The kid with the orange vest is kneeling beside me. I reach up and rub my eyes, the fog still not clearing. It's like someone turned down the transparency on his image. He's much clearer than he used to be. When I put my hands down again, he is still there. Still looks real. "I'm Thomas. You can hear me, right?"

I nod. His mouth definitely moved in time with those words. Thomas. He has a name.

"Good." His smile flashes across his face. "I'm sorry I couldn't save you. That's not really allowed. But I didn't want you to be alone. It's going to be alright."

Save me? What is he talking about?

I remember the backpack and the car horn. I sit up and look toward the intersection. There are emergency vehicles and cops everywhere. There are cones set up, flares in the road, and a single white sheet draped in the crosswalk.

"Oh my God." My voice is nothing more than a whisper. I jump to my feet and run right out into the road. But something's not right. I'm not running. I can't feel the pavement underneath me. I push the thought out of my mind and go to the nearest officer. "Can you help me?" I ask. Nothing. My voice doesn't even register. It's like he can't see or hear me.

Thomas is at my side in a flash. "It's going to be alright," he says. "I promise." He shoves his hands back in his pockets, that pose I've seen so many times. "It takes some getting used to, but at least you're not alone. I'll help you."

"Am I —?" I point at the sheet, unable to finish that last word.

He shrugs. "You and me both."

"And you knew I was going to —" I gulp in place of that word. It's too hard to imagine saying it. Somehow, that would make it more real.

He nods grimly.

"You're a ghost," I say.

"Right." He widens his eyes at me as if daring me to finish the thought.

I gulp down my nerves. "I am too?" My voice ticks up at the end, turning the statement into a question.

Thomas nods again. "But I'll help you figure it all out, I promise. Are you ready to go?" He holds out his hand to me, stretching those fingers between us delicately.

I turn and look back over my shoulder, taking in the sheet and the medical personnel all around. Then, I turn back to Thomas, place my hand inside his, and let him lead me into my next life.

Unthinkable

By now you likely know that I have an overactive imagination. It is constantly going in a ton of directions at once, good and bad. Sometimes stories come from that. In this case, a short story was born out of a worst fear. One that begs the question, who can you trust in a crisis?

et's just get out of the car and into the house. That's all I can think of as I'm pulling onto my street. The house comes into view, the garage door opening. The backseat of the seven-passenger vehicle is filled with four children, all of their school stuff, and so much noise my head is pounding. We are eight miles from the school. That's long enough for countless arguments about everything from our evening plans, of which we have none, to whether it will rain this weekend. Two eighth graders, a fourth grader, and a third grader crammed into one car always seems like a better idea than it really is. Especially on early release days. I just need to get into the house, where they'll have more space to move their elbows and separate from each other. Enough room for all of us to breathe.

I pull the car into the driveway and wait while the two on the passenger side climb out. Once I get this monstrosity of a vehicle into the garage there won't be room for them to open their doors. There's arguing about who gets to push the button to fold the center seat, allowing for the youngest to climb out of the third row. She always insists on sitting in the third row. She's still fascinated by the fact that there is a third row in this car we've only been driving for six thousand miles.

There, they're out. They rush into the house, eager to be first into the door. There's grumbling from the kid still in the back seat because they don't get to be first to see the dog. No one told you to stay in the car. I think it, but I don't yell it. We're almost in. No point in starting an argument now.

I get the car pulled up enough for the garage door sensors to tell me the door is capable of closing. I put on the emergency brake and turn the key. The back door flies open. The other young one escapes, runs out into the driveway, and promptly throws herself on the ground. "What are you doing?" I don't know why I'm asking her that. It's pretty obvious what she's doing. I shake my head. Be clear. "Come inside."

"No," she yells. Her voice echoes off the house across the street. She crosses her arms underneath the little rainbow emblem on her shirt. Her backpack shifts with the effort. "I'm staying out here."

I sigh. "For a little bit. I'm going inside and I'm closing the garage door. I'll unlock the front door so you can come back in that way." She's frustrated, I see that. I don't want to push her right now. It was an early release day. She's two hours ahead of schedule on homework already. That's the way I choose to think about it.

I head inside, close the garage door, open the front door, get a drink of water, and get the others started on the homework they told me about in the car. It takes maybe five minutes. The dog is stationed by the front door, and I scratch his ears as I walk by. I step out into the driveway, taking a long drink from my water.

I don't immediately see her. She's not there, on the ground pouting about their latest fight. I call her name as I walk toward the side of the house. There's no answer and she's not there.

My heart thuds in my chest. I call her name louder. I try to keep myself calm but my fingers are tingling. Panic, that's what this is.

I'm still holding the stupid glass of water when I start speed walking down the street, toward the mailboxes. I'm not sure what else to do. I'm calling her name and the condensation from the glass is slipping down over my fingers. I make it to the end of the street without seeing anything. I never hear her answer, I never see her backpack or her little head of brownish curly hair. I turn back around, running now, heading toward my house again. The water sloshes over the rim of the glass and all over my legs as it makes its way to the ground. I barely register it.

When I reach the house, I fling the screen door open. It smacks against the house, pausing the argument of the other three. "Have you seen Keira?" I shout. My voice is too loud, my panic taking over.

Their puzzled looks answer me before they can. No, they haven't seen her since we got home. "Put your shoes on. We need to find her."

I grab the leash for the dog. He's not a trained search dog, but he loves her too. Maybe he can help. Maybe he can't, but I'm panicking and I don't know what else to do. I tell myself there are plenty of places to search. We live close to the middle of our street. I've only checked in one direction. I haven't gone around the block. She was so mad when I left her outside, she had to have run off. I don't let myself consider another possibility. It can't be.

We are all outside now. The door is locked. The oldest wants to know what happens if she walks back while we're outside. That's a good point. He keeps his cell phone on him, to call me, and stations himself there at the front door. He's calm in a crisis, my oldest. That's awesome. I tell myself to be proud of that when there's time.

We set off walking, me and the dog on one side of the street and the kids on the other. We're all calling her name. People are outside now, asking what's going on. I try to stay calm, asking if they've seen a little girl. I describe her, blue leggings and a gray shirt with a rainbow emblem, a white backpack with pink accents, and brown hair. They know who I'm talking about but no one has seen her this afternoon.

By the time I get to the end of the street, I'm about to lose it. Keeping my voice calm, I tell the kids to jog back to the house. "It'll be ok. I'm just going to make a phone call." They look like they want to argue, but they don't. That's how I can tell they're really scared. They normally argue about everything.

I dial 9-1-1. "What is your emergency?" the voice asks. I'm almost shocked they really ask that. It almost makes this feel surreal. If I just focus on that voice, I can pretend this isn't happening. It's a terrible dream. Except it's not and I need help. I take a shaky breath. I can feel tears on my cheeks. I didn't even know I was crying.

"My niece is missing," I say. I'm not sure if my voice is loud enough. "She was sitting in the driveway when I went inside to get a drink of water. She's not there now. She's not answering when I call her. We walked up and down the street. I can't find her anywhere."

"OK, try to stay calm. What time did she go missing?"

"A few minutes ago." I think about how much I've done since I opened that door. I look at my watch and try to judge how long it's been since I picked them up from school. "Maybe ten minutes?"

"Okay, how old is the child?"

"She's nine." Oh God, she's only nine.

"Let me send an officer to you. What is your location?"

I ramble off my address as I walk back to the house. Even with the dog pulling on the leash and my focus on the phone call, I'm scanning the street for her. My chest feels tight, constricted.

I hang up the phone and groan. Compared to what I have to do now, that was the easy part. I hit the recent calls and tap the second one down. "What's up?" my sister answers.

Oh God, I can't do this. I have the urge to hang up. I'm the responsible one, the strong one. I don't make mistakes. Not like this. I can't find my voice. "I…" I have to tell her. Spit it out.

"You're scaring me, what's up?" I hear something shift. I imagine she's shutting her office door, settling back down. She's steeling herself up to hear bad news. "Is someone hurt?"

"I don't know. No. Oh God, please don't hate me. I … Keira is missing."

There's a pause, a long one. I anticipate yelling. I squeeze my eyes shut. "Where are you?" she asks.

That's not what I was expecting. She sounds scared and small. Not angry. "Home." I shake my head to clear it. "I'm on my street, we're looking. I called the police and they're on their way. We were at home, she was in the driveway. I left her outside for like five minutes while I got a drink. I don't know where she went. She has to be here somewhere." My voice cracks. "Oh my God, what was I thinking? I left her outside. She was upset, she was pouting. Where would she have gone? Where does she go when she's sad?"

My sister follows all of it, I know she does. She's one of the only people capable of following my thought process like breadcrumbs through my subconscious. "Um …" she's doing the same thing I did. I recognize the pauses, I can picture the head shakes. She doesn't believe it. "Maybe my house?" Now it's her turn to panic. I can feel my own panic fleeing, my spine straightening. We don't both panic at the same time, that's not what we do. My resolve grows just as I turn into my driveway, the other three kids nervously pacing and wringing their hands. "I need to leave, let me call my husband. I'll call my neighbor too. He can check at my house. I'm like forty minutes away. I'll drive fast. Call me the second the police arrive. Or when you find her. I'm on my way," she says into the phone. I hear the sounds of the door opening again, the noise of her office trickling in.

"The boys will bike ride down to your house, in case she's walking." I look at the boys when I say it, and they both give me a thumbs up. My son takes the dog leash. They unlock the door and lead the dog inside. I hear the door slam behind them. "We'll wait right here for the police. Come to my house unless I call you back. We'll find her." I smile at my daughter. It's not a real smile but I hope it helps her feel better. She's crying. "We'll find her."

"Yeah, I know. I'll call you back." My sister hangs up.

I put my phone in my pocket just as the garage door comes up. The boys are walking their bikes toward me. "We'll just be on the main road," my son says.

"You both have your phones?"

"Yeah." They hop onto the bikes and start pedaling.

"Be safe. If anything looks out of place or makes you nervous, turn around and come right back. Don't be a hero," I yell. I don't know what I mean, but I have to say something. They've made that bike ride countless times. It's about a mile between our houses. For teenage boys that's an easy distance to cover to see your best friend. They've made the ride at dusk, with adults and alone, in the rain, in the heat, and once one of them even made it carrying a dishwasher rack. But this time, I'm nervous. Maybe even more nervous than the first time I ever let them ride it. Because this time I'm afraid to let them out of my sight. I wish I had an alternative.

I take my phone back out of my pocket and call my husband. He answers on the second ring. "Hello, beautiful." His cheery voice brings tears to my eyes. I want to be that relaxed. I want to rewind thirty minutes, back to the car fighting before today went to hell. Before this nightmare. I feel my tears start again.

I turn away from my daughter so she doesn't see the tears. I frantically wipe at them. "Keira is missing."

"What?"

"She's missing. We got home from school and she refused to come inside. I let her stay outside. She was pouting. I went in and got some water then went out to check on her. She was gone. I can't find her."

"Where did she go?"

"If I knew that she wouldn't be missing," I yell.

I close my eyes and take a deep breath. I look over my shoulder to check on my daughter. She looks terrified. I kneel and pull her close to me, hugging her. She puts her head on my shoulder and I feel the little tremble of tears. "I'm sorry I yelled, I'm scared. I don't know. Do you have suggestions? Can you come home, please? I called the police already and they're on the way. But I think more adults on hand will help. Please."

"Of course. Let me talk to my boss. I'll be there. Give me an hour. Check the park, that's my only suggestion. We'll find her. I love you."

I nod, then remember he can't see that. "Yeah, ok. Thanks. I love you too."

I hang up and return the phone to my pocket. I wrap my arms around my daughter, tighter. I hold on because I need to. I squeeze because I have no other choice. What have I done?

The police arrive before the boys have called to say they're at my sister's house. One car, a nice-looking woman with her dark hair pulled in a tight bun at the base of her skull. "Good afternoon, ma'am. I understand we had a missing child." She smiles down at my daughter. "I'm glad to see she's returned. Is she alright?"

It takes me a second to process the mistake. "What? No. This is my daughter. My niece is missing." I pull out my phone again, open the photos, and find one of them together. Side by side, arms wrapped over shoulders. I point to Keira. "This is her." I run through the description of the outfit again. Tell the story that makes me feel terribly neglectful.

The phone rings. The screen lights up with a picture of my son. "I need to take this. They were bike riding down to check for her at her house." The policewoman nods and I swipe to answer. "Hello, did you find anything?"

"No, she's not here," my son answers. He sounds out of breath like he made that ride faster than he should've. I love him for that.

"Did you see anything unusual on the way there? Does anything look out of place at the house?" I don't want to ask about her backpack or shoes. I don't want them to have seen those things.

"No. We didn't see any people or kids at all."

"The park?" I remember what my husband suggested. The boys would've ridden right by there. "Was there anyone at the park?"

"Nope. We checked."

"Ok, hang on." I put the phone down by my side. "They didn't see anything on the way there or at her house. Should I have them come home?" I ask the policewoman, needing someone else to make this decision for me.

She nods. "Yes, that's fine."

Back to the phone. "Alright, come on home.

I'll see you in a few minutes. Keep your phones on. Be safe." I hang up and turn my attention back to her. My daughter sits on the ground, her knees pulled up to her chest. She is still softly crying. "What do we do now?"

"Honestly it's entirely too early to put her in as a missing person. We have a little leeway because of her age, but not much. Here's what I can do. I'm going to drive around the area and look for her. Maybe I'll get lucky and find her hiding. I'll check a few of the other parks in the area."

"Thank you, I appreciate that." I give her my cell phone number so she can call me with updates. She gives me her name and her badge number, just for my records. I don't write them down. I have a feeling I'm going to have trouble forgetting the details of today for the rest of my life.

The boys arrive back and we take care to put the bikes back where they go. I make them all come inside, try for some semblance of normal to keep them calm even though I'm losing my mind. They have drinks of water. They each have an apple. I'm wondering if Keira is thirsty or hungry. It's only been an hour.

My sister arrives only about five minutes before my husband. Her husband pulls up shortly after that. There are tears, lots of them. They all go off in different directions, calling and searching. I stay with the kids. I can't handle this. I feel myself slipping into a numb state like I'm watching this all on television. It's not real. I didn't let this happen.

I'm standing at the front door, watching the sidewalk and hoping for her little brown curls to magically appear in front of me. It's been about eighty minutes but they have stretched out to feel like a year. The police car pulls back up to the curb. I turn around and address the three sitting in the living room behind me. They all have backpacks open and papers strewn around them but no one is working. They're faking it, just like I am. "I'm stepping out front to talk to the police officer. Stay here."

When I turn back around emotion overwhelms me. I drop to my knees right there in the living room, hand outstretched toward the doorknob. Keira is being helped out of the back of the police car by the officer I recognize. My son steps to my side to see what is causing this reaction and bellows her name. He reaches right over me, opening the front door. Keira smiles awkwardly. She looks ... fine. Unharmed. Exactly the same way she looked when I saw her last. She doesn't look dirty, hurt, or upset.

I stand because the rest of the children want to get out to Keira and I'm blocking the doorway. The police officer puts her hand on Keira's shoulder and guides her toward the front door. "Look who I found," she says.

The children wrap Keira up in a giant four-person hug that I don't think I've ever seen this crew do before. For that second it's easy to believe the fighting will be a part of their past, along with this story. Something they remember but don't talk about. Something they grow out of.

"I don't have the full story for you of where she was, although I'm curious," the police officer explains to me in a quiet voice. "She was sitting by the side of the main road there," she gestures in the direction of my sister's house. "She had her backpack on her lap and was hunting for something. She's not a big talker though and didn't want to tell me where she'd been. I'm hoping you can get some more information from her. Could you try for me?"

I slowly register what she's saying. Keira was by the road. The road my son and nephew had already checked. The road the police officer had probably driven down a few times in her search. The message she's not openly saying is that Keira was definitely not in that same spot the entire time. So where was she? I look down at the group of hugging cousins and realize I need the answer. Because if someone took her, a possibility I wouldn't let myself even think about until right now, that's a spot where they may have dumped her. But she looks unharmed, she looks fine.

"Alright, everyone, give her some room. Inside, please." The children, reluctantly, break back apart. I usher the other three with gentle hands on their heads. "Inside, please." They shuffle inside. I smile down at Keira, crouch to her level, and open my arms. She rushes into my arms, almost knocking me over with enthusiasm. My chest feels full of happiness, like it will burst out of me. I stay like that, holding her, inhaling her scent. She still smells the same and I start to feel like I am strong enough to do this. Then I pull back and look at her little face. "Where have you been, kiddo?" I ask.

"I went for a walk."

"A walk?" She nods. "Where did you walk?"

She points down my street, toward her house. "That way," she says.

I catch eyes with the policewoman over Keira's head. She's smiling as if this is good news. I'm not as easy to convince. "Did you walk by yourself?"

Keira scrunches her eyes at me. It's a look I recognize. She thinks I've lost my marbles. "Yes."

"You scared everybody," I tell her. "We didn't know where you were."

"That's what the police lady said. I'm sorry. I just wanted to go home and be by myself."

Except she wasn't home. We looked there. We sent the boys there. My sister called the neighbor. Shit, my sister. I pat Keira on the head and stand up.

"I need to call my sister and tell her we found her. What else do you need from us? Thank you so much, by the way."

"Call her, I'll wait." The officer pats Keira on the back. "Do you want to get a drink of water inside? I bet the boys can help you."

I take my phone out of my pocket as Keira opens the front door and makes her way inside. I hit my sister's number. I don't even think it rings before she answers. "Hello?"

"She's here. She's at my house. She looks fine."

"Oh thank God." I hear her echo the information to someone, presumably her husband. "We'll be right there." There's a soft click, telling me she disconnected. I tap on my husband's picture and repeat the information to similar results.

Then I hang up the phone. "They're all on their way back here. Thank you, again, for finding her."

"The thing is," the officer says, frowning, "she wasn't there the entire time. I don't think I need the exact route she took because she doesn't appear to have suffered trauma and she appears to be unharmed. This seems like it happened exactly as she's telling you. She walked away, maybe got lost, and then sat down somewhere and that's when I found her. But you should ask her to show you where she went when things calm down. If it were me, I'd want to know."

I nod along as if that's my decision to make. That's my sister's territory. I can't fathom a world where I'd be the responsible one allowed to make those kinds of decisions again. I, clearly, don't know what's best for anyone. Keira might have been the one to walk away but I can't stop thinking that I did this. I took my eyes off her. If I had followed her out of the car, sat beside her on the driveway, put my arm around her, and listened, this would all go away. How do I move past that?

I watch the rest of the scenes play out as if I'm a bystander. The adults all return, driving too fast for the street we live on. They rush past the police officer into the house where they reunite with Keira. I hear my sister chastise her for wandering off. They make their way back out to talk to the officer who, true to her word, waits for all of them as if she doesn't have a packed schedule to deal with. As if this once missing and now found child is the most important part of her day. I hear her tell Keira's parents the same thing she told me. I watch my sister process that, tears slipping down her face. I wonder if she even realizes she's still crying.

At some point, things move on. The police officer leaves. My sister takes her family home. My family comes back inside. My husband makes dinner.

The act of being normal is playing out before me in real-time.

But inside I still feel like an imposter. Because I let this happen. I wonder if I will ever forgive myself for this. It doesn't feel likely.

Stranger Promises

I was a teacher for a long time. During that time I saw a lot of students come and go through my classroom doorway. Many of them enjoyed writing. Many of them enjoyed reading. We talked about stories often. Once, a student who enjoyed talking about books with me asked me why none of the cool paranormal experiences ever happened to girls like her. That stayed with me. So when I decided this short story needed to be told, I put a girl who reminds me of that student into the starring role. As you read, think about this: Would you trust yourself to have integrity?

I'm the fat girl in my high school.

I already lost some of you. Half the ones I lost angrily flipped the page to skip my story because they couldn't believe I called myself fat. They don't want to read a story about a girl who they assume has low self-esteem. The other half made a face and flipped because they were disgusted with me for being fat. You? Well, you're still here. So let's get on with it.

I'm the girl at school who seems to be referred to only by her weight. The conversations often sound like this:

"Did you hear what happened with Alice?"

"Who's Alice?"

"The fat girl in your bio class. The one who drives a Prius."

See, both of those things define me whether I like it or not. They also both happen to be true. But, just once, I'd like to see it flipped. I'd like to be the girl who sometimes drives the Prius her mother bought from a used car lot who also just happens to be fat. Instead of the other way around. Or, even better, I'd like someone to find some other way of describing me.

"Who's Alice?"

"The cute brunette with the great ass, the nice Vans, and the pineapple print backpack."

All of those things happen to be true too, if you ask me. Still, I don't see that happening anytime soon. Case in point? The article buried on page 3 of today's school newspaper. Here, let me show you.

Class of 2024 Achievement Award Nominees Announced

Perhaps you've heard of Alice Redman and Sofia Waters. Alice is a friendly economist who is always championing body positivity for overweight teens like herself. Sofia is the student body president who is currently holding a 4.0 GPA. On the surface, the two girls have nothing in common. At least until today. Today the nominees were announced for the annual Achievement Award and these two are the sole nominees.

The school has a history of awarding one incoming senior with the prestigious honor. The Achievement Award comes with a plaque, honor cords to wear at graduation, and a $300 cash prize to be used on a charitable project of their choice.

While it may be surprising to see two such different personalities nominated, the fact is one of them will be earning those prizes in just four short weeks. Congratulations on being nominated, ladies, and may the best woman win.

"Overweight teens like herself." Did you catch that? They couldn't resist. So, deny it if you want, but I'm the fat girl. Here's where my mind is today, do I have a chance of earning that award? When one of the main things people say about you is that you're fat, can they ever see you as anything else? Discuss.

***

"Alice!" I recognize the bellow. It's the hearty full-lung call of a person who is practiced in throwing their voice long distances through hallways, across packed gymnasiums, and over morning announcement microphones. Sofia Waters. The other nominee for the Achievement Award this year and, by default, my competition.

I spin around and face the bellower head-on. "Sofia, you rang?"

She jogs up to me and stops inches from a collision. "I just wanted to offer my congratulations for your nomination." She holds her hand out between us like I'm supposed to shake it. Then she tilts her head, waiting for the obligatory return congrats.

"Yeah, thanks. I hope I get it." I'm not playing her game today. I don't want to stand here in the hallway and do this whole "you're more deserving, no YOU'RE more deserving" show for the underclassmen filtering by us. I just want to go to class and move on with my life. Is that too much to ask?

"Aren't you going to congratulate me, too?" she asks, dropping her hand to her side.

Apparently, it was too much to ask. I sigh. "Look, we both know this is probably already decided somewhere by some committee. I don't want to spend our time pretending like we both want the other person to stand a fair shot. I want it, you want it. End of."

She rolls her eyes. "You don't have to be a bitch about it."

Oh, but I do. Because the truth is, whether I

like it or not, I'm never getting that award. Can you imagine the school deciding to put some nobody like me in the paper to represent them for the charity of my choice, which would be the Eating Disorder Association? That would mean linking their school to a fat teen who is obviously, based on the charity she chose, comfortable talking about body weight and appearance in a way they are absolutely not. Don't get me wrong, I want this award. It's why I applied. I have great ideas about bringing in a body-positive workshop for our school and for getting a body-positive counselor for the athletic department. I mean, every single student has to meet a physical education component, that would be the perfect place to introduce body-positive training. It's a missed opportunity, for sure. The problem is, although I like the idea, I'm sure it's not going to win against whatever Sofia the perfect has planned. "I have to go to class," I tell her. "See you around."

***

Despite Sofia stopping me in the hallway, I manage to slip in the door of my sign language class before it shuts. The teacher smiles at me from his perch at the front of the room. "Made it," I call. He shoots me a thumbs up and I take my seat. I don't have much time to think (read: stress) about the award while I'm in class. We're deep into the material at this point so most of our class is spent communicating with hand movements. Classical music softly emits from the speakers near the teacher's desk, but otherwise, it is quiet.

We're almost to the end of the period before the teacher makes his way near my desk and signs "congratulations".

I don't realize what he is talking about at first, completely focused on the conversation my partner and I had been having to practice our study words. Then it all rushes back. The award, the newspaper article, my practically non-existent chances of winning. "Thank you," I sign and say.

He then signals us to go ahead with our practice. My partner seems fine but I stumble a few times over signs that I know. The teacher corrects me once. When he walks off, my partner leans close and whispers, "I always get more nervous with an audience too." Like that is supposed to make me feel better. All it does is confirm that someone else noticed that I screwed up. I sigh. Thankfully, the bell rings before I'm forced to answer anything else.

In the hallway, I meet up with Erik. We've been friends since we were both tiny. He used to live directly across the street, making us friends by association. Then his family moved and we were separated in elementary and middle school.

Thankfully, we're back together in the same high school and have been friends again since the day I spotted him across the campus when we were freshmen. "That class period was bullshit," Erik says, falling into step beside me as we head towards our next class together. "Remind me again why I still have a full schedule even though I'm a Junior?"

"Because you love driving me to and from school and you don't want me to be alone?" I say. I loop my arm through his and we walk elbow-and-elbow in the hallway. "Plus you feel immensely sorry for me that too many extracurriculars in my early high school career led me to have a full stupid schedule my Junior year to compensate and graduate on time."

"Right, right. I forgot." He lightly bumps my hip with his as we walk. "By the way, saw your name in the paper this morning."

I roll my eyes. "Did you catch them calling me fat?"

"They did not use the F-word," Erik says. I can almost hear the matching eye roll in his voice. "They were very careful to avoid that word, actually."

"They always are," I laugh a little. "Anyway, can you give me a ride after school or am I walking?" I don't care either way, he knows that, but I want to change the subject before Erik starts talking about how the people at this school don't care about my weight and that the preconceived notion I have that they do is all in my head. It's hogwash and I don't want to have that discussion again. He'll never change my mind and I'll never change his. End of.

"I have to pick my mom up right away so I can't. Unless you want to come with me." He smiles hopefully.

I hate driving all the way to central Phoenix with Erik to pick his mother up. I shake my head. "No go, man. I'll walk. Thanks though. What about tomorrow?"

"No car tomorrow. She needs it for some lunch meeting. Do you have the Prius tomorrow?"

"Still in the shop," I whine.

"We can walk together," Erik offers. He's close enough to meet up with me on my way to school if I take the right route.

I roll my eyes and sigh with a dramatic flourish. "That'll have to work."

***

Erik wasn't kidding about having to rush out to get his mom right after school. He barely has time to wave at me while he's jogging to the parking lot. I give a half-hearted wave back and turn my feet toward the east side of campus. If I have to walk home, I may as well cut through the fields and landscaped areas instead of sticking to the street. I may save a few minutes that way and every minute counts in this heat.

I make it about a block before I realize the heat is even worse than I thought. It is back way too soon this year. We should've had another month or so before it was this unbearable. I decide to duck into the little restaurant on the corner coming up and get myself a drink for the walk home. I slip my arm out of my backpack strap on one side so I can pull it around to the front of me and dig around in the smallest pocket. I find three single dollars rolling around in there. That's enough. I shove everything back in and readjust my backpack as I step onto the walkway to the store.

There are a few people from the school inside when I pull the door open. I don't know those kids, not by name, but I recognize a few of the faces and I definitely recognize the emblem on the t-shirt two of the boys are wearing. Football players, likely. Great, just what I need. I make it my mission to get to the counter as quickly as possible. I order myself the lemon-lime soda which always seems more refreshing even though it's just as sugar-packed as the darker stuff, and stand off to the side to wait for it.

I hear the boys at the table laugh a little and I take a deep breath. I assume they're laughing at me.

One of them probably recognized me from school. Or they just like making fun of all the people they see out in the real world who aren't as fit as them. Who knows? It's not worth my time or energy so I'm not asking.

The lady approaches the counter and hands me my drink. I take it with a grateful smile and hustle back towards the door I came in.

I'm being so careful not to look up at the football table that I literally almost crash into a man coming in the door. He holds out his hands. "Whoa, in a hurry there young lady?"

"Shit, sorry. I wasn't watching where I ..." My voice trails off because this guy is cute. He's a little taller and a little older than me, but not too much of either. He has these dark eyes that almost seem to sparkle with something that makes me think of starry nights by a campfire. He's dressed in all black, which matches his striking hair. The entire look just screams "I belong on a TV show." Then his whole face breaks out in a smile and I swear to everything holy I feel like I'm melting right there in the cheap, shitty little restaurant.

"You're good," he says. "You didn't run into me." He leans down toward me and winks. An actual wink. "At least, not yet." Then he straightens back up. "You need anything before I step out of your way?"

"What? No." I stutter, distracted by this

adorable specimen.

"If you say so." He takes a step to his left and holds out his right hand like an invitation for me to glide by him. I risk a glance at the amount of room he's left. Even if I turn sideways there's no way I am getting between him and the little hightop table next to him. I blush and turn sideways anyway so I'm fully facing him as I try to make my way between them. I feel the table cut into my back and he is so close. Like too close, almost. He whispers, "Are you sure there's nothing you need? No desires? No deep wishes?"

"What?" I mutter, pausing. "That's a weird fucking thing to say."

He laughs and the sound is soft, his breath passing by my cheek. "Everyone needs a favor sometimes. Maybe something at school you were hoping for."

A strange feeling climbs my spine. Who is this guy? Doesn't it sort of sound like he's implying he knows about the contest? But he can't, right? I shake my head. "No way, I'm good. I don't take random offers of help winning school contests from some stranger at a fast food place." I make my way past him and keep my eyes firmly focused on the main door of the restaurant. "I'm good, but thanks."

"So there is something," he calls. His voice is so sugar-sweet that I can't help but turn my head a little toward it. It's enough to see that beautiful face again. The eyes practically pull my attention to him. He winks again. "Are you sure I can't be of some assistance?"

I throw all my energy into a laugh, making it sound as deep as possible. I don't know what's going on with this guy but I intend to prove to him that I think he's ridiculous. "Yeah, sure, whatever." I roll my eyes and cross the distance to the door. I push it open and throw one last look behind me. He's still there, still watching me, those eyes still sparkling. I shake my head. "Weirdo."

Then I'm back outside, trying to forget that entire interaction. Those guys from school saw that too, right? None of them thought it was strange enough to warrant a quick interruption.

I stop walking as the realization rushes over me. They put him up to it. Those dickheads got some sexy stranger to creep me out. They're probably friends of Sofia's or something. Maybe they just wanted to mess with me. I resume walking, determined to let it go. If this was a prank I refuse to let those assholes know it worked by showing my fear. I will write it off as a prank and let it go.

***

"How was your evening?" Erik asks the next

morning as he falls into step beside me at the corner on my way to school.

I roll my eyes. "Totally boring. Yours?"

He shrugs. "Fine. Mom made some new recipe and it was practically inedible. Couldn't bring myself to tell her though." He holds up a plastic bag. "Remind me to tell her I lost this somewhere and throw it in the first available dumpster."

I laugh. "Oh, I didn't even tell you about the walk home. I stopped for a soda, right?"

"Sounds legit."

"There were some football players there and they talked some total stranger into this weird thing where he offered me some help with a problem."

Erik's facial expression is more fitting for someone trying to understand a foreign language than my best friend trying to understand what I'm telling him happened. "What the hell are you talking about?" he says. "Back up."

"Some guy came up to me at the store and asked me what I needed his help with. I don't remember how he worded it, just that it was super weird. I said I didn't need help and he asked if there wasn't something at school that I was hoping for. Something like that. He knew about it. They had to have told him, right?"

"What makes you think these particular guys are the ones that put this stranger up to something?"

I shrug. "They were there. Wouldn't they want to see the results of their little prank first-hand?"

"So they were talking to him before and he walked up to you?"

I think back and shake my head. "No, he came in the door just before we ran into each other."

"When would they have put him up to this?" Erik asks. I can tell by the tone of his voice that he's not buying this. Honestly, saying it out loud makes me realize how weak it is. But why else would that total stranger have talked to me at all, never mind offered me some kind of sketchy deal? No, they had to have put him up to it.

I wave my hand in the air like I'm swatting away his doubts. "Whatever, I don't know all the details but I know they did this. It was stupid and immature which is totally them. I just need to make sure I don't let them know it bothered me."

Erik can't think of anything to say to that so he falls quiet. He stays that way, focusing on his footsteps and not talking about anything, all the way to school. When we step onto campus, he bumps me with his arm. "When did you have time for that?" he asks, pointing.

I turn my attention to the object, which appears to be a large pink poster with a gorgeous freehand outline drawing of my face on it. I step closer and read the text at the top of the poster. "Vote for Alice and bring a healthy focus to our PE curriculum" it boldly states. I turn around to Erik, my mouth agape. "I did not do this," I tell him. "You did, right?"

"Do I look like I knew to expect these?" he asks. He does not. He looks as shocked as I feel.

I turn to the picture again. Over my shoulder, Erik must be doing the same because he points to it. "Who drew this? It's fucking amazing."

"I have no idea." My voice comes out sort of breathy because I'm still trying to process what I'm seeing. The artwork looks original like someone drew it with pencils and just put it on the pink poster. It's all lines and shading, no color. It is unmistakably me but, also, beautiful. Trust me, that is not a word I use to describe myself often. But something about the way I'm looking off into the distance captures this focus that just looks amazing. "Do I look like that?" I ask, turning my head to match the pose.

Erik looks from me to the poster and back again repeatedly. "Completely. It's so amazing. I can't believe you don't know who did this." He slaps me on the shoulder. "Oh my God, could it be the guy who offered you help? Could he have done this?"

I roll my eyes. "Yes, of course. Why didn't I think of that? The guy I met for eight point three seconds yesterday was able to sketch me from memory and have posters of it made then rush down to our school, even though I didn't tell him what school we attended, and hang them up. All of this was done overnight."

"I suppose it's ridiculous." He sighs. "Whatever, someone did this. We need to put our energy into finding out who."

"Fine," I agree. "Ask around today. See if anyone recognizes the art or knows where these posters came from. We'll report back on our walk home."

***

By the end of the day, I've concluded exactly one thing: no one knows where the hell those posters came from. No one recognizes the art, although a lot of people comment on how amazing it is. Everyone assumes I put them up and seems confused when I say I didn't. I'm pretty sure a few people even think I'm lying about putting them up. "Tell me you've got something," I say when I see Erik walking up to me after school.

"Nothing. Rumor is that you did it yourself or that I did it and lied to you about it."

"That's still my theory," I joke.

Erik rolls his eyes and starts in the direction of our houses. "I don't have the kind of money you'd have to dump into a printing project like that," he points out. "Someone told me it's expensive to print posters that large and there's tons of them all over campus."

"Did you see the one in the cafeteria?" I ask. "I think it's larger than the ones in the hallways."

"I don't even know where to print those," Erik says. "Honest."

"I know." I bump him with my shoulder. "I trust you. This is just weird, right?"

"Really, really weird," he agrees.

We walk in silence for a bit. I'm not sure what Erik is thinking about but I am, for sure, trying to figure out this weird puzzle. Eventually, Erik cues me back into reality by clearing his throat. "I need a drink," he says. He points at the same restaurant where I stopped yesterday.

I freeze right there on the sidewalk because the guy from yesterday is also standing there, reclining against a handicapped parking sign with his hands shoved deep into his pockets like he's waiting for me. Erik, who hasn't stopped, has to turn around and come back a few steps to catch back up to me. He looks concerned. "What?" he prompts.

"That's the guy from yesterday." I point, not caring if I offend him by talking about him.

"No shit?" Erik looks and then whips his head back to me. "That hot guy is the guy from yesterday? Did you mention he was gorgeous? I feel like you left that out."

"Focus." I take a deep breath. "Let's go talk to him. You'll see how weird he is. You'll see what I meant." I don't wait for Erik to agree or argue. Instead, I stomp off in the direction of the restaurant with renewed purpose.

The guy pushes off the pole and smiles when I'm closer, confirming that he was, indeed, waiting for me. "Back again," he calls when I'm close enough to hear him. I keep walking until I am right up in his space. "I figured you'd be by today to thank me for what I'd done," he says.

"Who drew that picture?" I ask, cocking my hip to the side and planting my hand on it. I'm trying my hardest to look relaxed like this is no big thing. Really, my heart is pounding. Is it possible this guy did this in one night? It's not, right? But, still, something is telling me that is exactly what happened. He's responsible.

He smiles. "You like it?"

"I don't understand why you did it."

He winks, just like yesterday. "We had a deal. You need this from me now and I will come back later to collect a favor as payment."

"What?" I shake my head. "No, no way. I never said anything about a favor. Who the hell are you anyway?"

Erik lays a hand on my arm and pulls me back.

His hand shoots into the space between us and the stranger. "I'm Erik," he offers. "I don't think we met."

The man takes the offered hand and gives it a single pump up and down. "Charmed, I'm sure."

"Great. Why don't you lay out the terms of this favor for us both so that no one can accuse you later of being some kind of trickster? No secrets. Are you saying you put up campaign posters to help my friend here win her award?"

The man gives Erik only the briefest glance before his eyes are back on my face. "She needed something that I am capable of providing."

"Yeah, see, that's not really an answer," Erik pushes. Again, he puts his hand on my arm and pulls. Again, I take a step back. "You're being deceptive on purpose. Did you do this?"

The wink again. "Perhaps."

"Close enough," Erik says. "So I'm assuming you did this. What did you want in return?"

"As I said, the win now for a favor later."

"No, that's not how this works," Erik says. "You say out loud right now what Alice's part of the deal is or we're out. We aren't working with a trickster."

He leans closer, so his face is dangerously close to mine. "Oh, but you are. It's already begun," he whispers.

"No," I yell. He snaps his head back to its proper location. "I never agreed to anything. I laughed in your face. This is not happening." I gesture between us. "Whatever you think I agreed to is not happening. I'll pay you for the posters if I have to but this ends now."

"Are you sure? Think carefully, child. That win is not guaranteed. You're taking chances. I can remove the doubt for you."

This has gone on long enough. I turn my upper body toward the restaurant. "Why are we standing here listening to this whack job?" I ask. "Let's go inside. This is not happening." I force out a sort of laugh.

"Stop laughing," Erik says, pulling back on my arm again. "This is how people end up losing deals with the devil and dying or something."

I think of that old country song about dealing with the devil then turn my head so they can both see me roll my eyes. "Maybe I'll win a fiddle." I yank my arm away from Erik and take a step toward the door. "Let's go. This is done."

"You have to be clear," Erik says. "No gray areas. Guys like this thrive in gray areas."

I throw my hands up and groan. "Fine." I stomp the few steps back to the guy so that we're face to face again. "Look, I want to win but I want to win honestly because my project is good. I don't want to win with backhanded deals. No deal. Sorry I was confusing yesterday. I'm being clear today. We do not have a deal. You hear me? No. Deal."

He nods once, a slow sort of nod that somehow feels weightier than a regular nod. "Clear enough." Then he snaps his fingers. "Our agreement is dissolved."

I stop myself from saying we didn't have an agreement because that seems counterproductive at this point. Instead, I grab Erik and pull him into the restaurant. I don't stop directing him until we're at the counter. Then I let go. "What the hell was that?" Erik asks.

"I'm not sure if I want to know," I say. "Let's just forget about this and hope it all goes back to normal."

Erik looks skeptical but nods. "Yeah, ok. I'll try."

***

The rest of the month does, in fact, go by smoothly. The posters remain but slowly start to fall off or come down. At least, I assume that's what is happening because I see less and less of them. Things are so normal for so long that I almost forget about the weird interactions at the restaurant. Almost.

Our speeches in front of the student body go well. A lot of people seem to like what I say about my project, some even nod along. Honestly, Sofia's sounds good too. She's obviously put a lot of time and effort into it. If I didn't want to win so badly, I'd want her plan.

Just as our principal is explaining the voting process, I notice he's in the audience. The cute guy from the restaurant. Cold sweat breaks out on my arms. Is he here for me? Is there something I forgot to say or do? Was I not clear?

Oh my God, what if Sofia took him up on the offer? Is she about to win because of some underhanded deal with this guy? I try to remember if I've seen any posters for her that seem a bit beyond what you can make yourself. I can't think of any.

The principal dismisses everyone and I make a straight line to the stranger. "Why are you here?" I hiss. "Are you working with her?"

He laughs and the sound is somehow terrifying. When he stops, he looks down at me with another wink. "No. She never needed me. You were right about that. You didn't stand a chance but not for the reason you thought. Her proposal was better, it was always that simple."

"So why are you here?" I repeat. "I was clear, I don't want your help."

"Oh, it's too late for that now. I can admit when I was beaten. I wanted to swindle you, catch you when you needed something, and make it worth my time. You were right to trust yourself and that friend of yours." He takes a step back from me and crosses his arms. The gesture makes him look distant, somehow, like he's fading into the background. "If you ever decide you'll pay any cost for something, you know where to find me." His voice is so quiet now. "I'll be at the corner of your darkest thoughts and your most desperate times, waiting."

"Alice," a voice calls. I think it's Sofia.

I turn my head to the right just long enough to call out "One second." But that little turn of my head was enough. In my peripheral vision, I can already see that he's gone. An empty row of chairs stands in front of me. I look like I'm talking to no one. "What the —" I mumble.

Then, she's beside me. "Should we walk in together to vote?" Sofia asks. "I thought that would be kind of a cool gesture. I liked your proposal."

"Yeah, I liked yours too," I admit. I turn my head around in circles, looking for signs of the cute guy somewhere on the edges of the room.

Somehow, I'm not surprised when I can't find him. But I hear his words again in my head as if he is whispering in my ear. "I'll be at the corner of your darkest thoughts and your most desperate times, waiting."

The Only Chance You Get

This one will require little to no introduction so I'll merely say this: would you trust the people in your life to have your best interests at heart?

1996

Sonia holds the paperback in front of her face, pretending to be completely engrossed. She hopes no one can see her embarrassed flush, which she's sure is covering her entire neck and face. She's also hoping this makes her look so busy that no one will interrupt her. This entire experiment was a huge mistake. She can't believe she let Jeanne talk her into it. She wishes she could take it all back, but it's too late now. There are too many people in the classroom. When she dropped the paper, it was just her and the math teacher. Even the teacher, after giving her the perfunctory head nod, turned his back to her to write on the board. She's pretty sure he didn't care about the paper she dropped on a desk. But if she got up now everyone in this third-period class would see her retrieve it. She has no choice; she has to leave it.

She reads the first paragraph on this page again, attempting to focus on fictional worlds. The chatter at the door gets louder, the signal that someone new and cool is approaching the classroom. Sonia lowers her head even further, hiding behind the paperback. "Oh my God, I thought you were going to be absent or something," she hears. This voice belongs to Amanda. The most adorable girl ever to exist. If Amanda and Sonia were standing side-by-side no boy in their right mind would pay any attention to Sonia. At least, so far they haven't.

"Have I ever missed a day of this class?" Tom asks. Sonia, who would've thought her neck was already as low as it could go, drops her head further. She cannot believe she let Jeanne talk her into this. It was a really stupid plan.

Tom takes a second in the doorway to scan the room. His second-period class is on the other side of the school so he's usually the last person to make it to this class on time. It looks like today is no different. All twenty of the people he is used to sitting near for this advanced course are accounted for. A few are standing by the door. These kids are like flies. They hang out near whomever they think is the best for their social status at all times. They're nice enough and will boost your ego, but they have no real personality. He wonders if they even continue to exist when no one else is around, maybe they fade into the background like ghosts.

His eyes land on the desk he always sits in. Left half of the room but on the inner aisle. He says it's so he can stretch out his long legs, which he does, but it's really because that puts him center of the classroom and perfectly in front of the board. He plays his cool guy persona well at school, even when that means hiding what a good student he is.

Today, there's a small square of paper sitting on his desk. He squints and moves closer. Probably the paper was left by whoever sat there during second period. That happens all the time. It could be stray notes from their own class. It could be a stupid note that says "Hi, I sit here too." Or, it could be something juicier. Something dropped by accident that was not meant for his eyes. Something that gives him a little gossip he can use to his advantage. Everyone likes gossip. If he can feed the flies with someone new, they stop paying attention to every little detail of his life for a few days.

No such luck, he muses. The note on the desk has his name printed in light letters, perfectly spaced and even height. Someone who has near-perfect penmanship left him a note.

The bell rings. Mr. Zucker pushes himself up from behind his desk and waves his hand. "That's the bell. Take your seats." Tom drops into his chair and pulls a notebook out of his backpack. He opens the notebook to a blank page, spreads his single sheet of looseleaf with the homework problems over the top, and leaves the little note with his name visible underneath the pile. He plans to wait for a good moment to open it. Right now, during homework check time, too much attention is on the students. He wouldn't get away with it.

Zucker's voice gets louder. "I said take your seats." Tom looks up to see Amanda and a few of the other flies still standing. They're close to their usual seats, but they're taking their time. He wonders if they have seen the note and decides they likely have. That's why they were all waiting for him by the door. It's why they're moving slowly now. They're all waiting to see what he does with it. He pulls on the note just a little, so it's sticking out from below the notebook. He's hoping he communicated that he intends to wait to read it. They may as well sit.

As if cued by a conductor, they all drop into their chairs. Tom shakes his head. "Let's get started. Last night you were assigned twelve problems. We can go over as many as four right here on the board together. Who would like to see a problem worked out?" Zucker booms.

Amanda's hand flies up. "I'd like to see number seven, please."

There are groans from the class. The answers to the odd-numbered problems are in the back of the textbook. For that reason, the students know to only ask to see even numbered problems. This maximizes the number of answers you are sure are correct. Tom glances down at his paper. He did number seven and got the answer at the back.

While Zucker turns his attention to the board, showing the steps for solving the problem, Tom slips the paper out from underneath the notebook and into his lap. He carefully unfolds the paper, trying not to let it rustle. Inside, the handwriting is the same as the front. Light pencil marks are perfectly spaced and form uniform letters. No loopy cursive, no hearts over any letters. Just simple handwriting.

He squints a little at the light lettering.

Tom,
First, this was not my idea. I was perfectly fine with you going through our entire sophomore year without ever knowing this information. But, I've been talked into telling you. I think you're cute and I have a crush on you. I would bet money that you hear that all the time. Basketball fans must flock to you daily, gushing about how amazing you are. I'm sure it doesn't mean anything that some anonymous girl wants to tell you … again. But here's

the thing, I have never seen a basketball game. I don't think you're cute because of how you play. I like the way you look when you are talking about Shakespeare in English. I like the way you look when you're laughing with your friends at lunch. Anyway, enough embarrassing stuff. I just wanted you to know that someone sees the real you … and likes what they see. Have a nice day.

It's not signed. Tom looks up at the front of the room and sees that Zucker has moved on to solving number 10. He glances down at his homework paper and realizes he stopped solving that problem halfway through. Shit. He quickly shoves the note under his notebook again and focuses on the teacher. He copies the new steps and carefully boxes the answer he can't believe he didn't get on his own.

"Alright, enough free answers," Zucker booms in that loud voice only he can get away with using in the classroom. "Take out your notes."

Tom passes his homework sheet forward. Then he leans to his left. "Hey, did you see who dropped this?" he whispers to the kid beside him. This kid's name is Jeff, Tom knows. He is ridiculously smart and thinks he is invisible. He listens to great music choices and could be a great addition to the soccer team if he liked sports. He's the kind of guy Tom imagines he would be friends with in another reality. One where he's allowed to be who he wants to be instead of who he's supposed to be. Jeff nods and points toward the front of the room to a girl with a long ponytail and terrible posture. She looks like she is trying to sink into the little plastic chair underneath her. "Thanks," Tom whispers before straightening back up.

He spends the rest of the class period taking careful notes, trying not to think about the letter, paying attention to the teacher as best as he can, and trying not to sneak peeks at the girl who dropped the letter. He knows her name is Sonia. He knows she shares five of the classes on his schedule. She definitely isn't one of the flies, which is pretty obvious from her letter and her behavior. She doesn't seem to care what anyone thinks of her. Honestly, before today he hadn't given her a second thought. Now he can't seem to stop thinking about her long enough to pay attention to the math notes he is supposed to be writing.

The bell rings and Tom scrambles to stuff the notebook back in his bag. Usually, he's packed and ready before that bell rings. He can't believe he was sitting here daydreaming. He rushes out of the door, the note in his clenched fist. She's at least three people ahead of him, walking in the same direction he needs to go. He rushes. "Sonia," he calls. "Hang on, wait a second."

Sonia stops and looks over her shoulder, her

eye creased in confusion. When she spots him, a blush takes over her entire face. She whips back around and continues walking. "Wait, hang on a second," he calls.

When she pulls to the left and steps out of the flow of traffic under an overhang, he hurries to catch up. He pulls the note out of his back pocket. "I wanted to ask you about this," he says. He's surprised to find his embarrassment is strong. What if it was a joke? What if she didn't mean any of it? It does seem odd that she would know exactly what he was thinking. "Is this, maybe, from you?" he asks.

Sonia doesn't even look at it. She shakes her head from left to right and drops her eyes to the ground. "No," she whispers.

"Are you sure? Jeff thought he saw you put it —"

"It's not mine," she says, more vehemently. "Sorry."

Something about the way she is refusing to look at the note makes him wonder if she is lying. He slips the note back in his pocket. "Alright, but do you maybe know who put it there? It's really flattering. I'd just like to find the girl."

Her blush deepens but she shakes her head again. "I have no idea. It wasn't me. I have to go to class." Then she's gone, rushing off into the sea of kids crowding the outdoor walkways.

Tom shrugs and walks off. He wonders if he will ever know where this note came from.

Page 93

2024

The knocking at the door startles Sonia enough to make her drop the cell phone she's holding onto her lap. It makes a soft thudding noise against the comforter. "Who in the hell?" she mumbles. She picks up the cell phone again to check the time. 6:27 AM. Who would be knocking on her door before seven in the morning on a random Wednesday?

She throws the covers back, puts on her slippers, and makes her way across the condo to the front door. She checks the peephole before smiling and throwing the door open. Jeff is standing there, dressed for work, and holding a bag in his hand. "I heard you were out sick yesterday and I know that means you probably didn't eat. So I figured I'd show up a little early. I brought some essentials." He holds up a hot takeout cup from the coffee shop down the street. "First offering, caffeine."

"Oh, my hero," Sonia says, reaching for the cup. "Come in, it's cold out there."

"Thanks."

Sonia takes a step back and takes a sip from the cup as he makes his way inside. Mocha, light on chocolate syrup so it actually tastes like coffee, absolutely no whipped cream. He always gets her order exactly right. "You're seriously the best."

Jeff crosses her apartment with all the confidence of a best friend who has been here hundreds of times. He drops the bag onto the table and produces a croissant, a chocolate-covered donut, something that is probably a pumpkin donut, and a blueberry muffin. "Two for you and two for me. You get the first choice."

He slips off his jacket, laying it on the back of the chair closest to him while Sonia pretends to ponder. They both know exactly what her first choice will be. "Chocolate donut is mine."

"Good," he slides it off to one side. "I'll take the pumpkin one and won't feel guilty about it at all." He pushes it to the other side of the table. "Second choice?"

Sonia scrunches her nose, thinking. The blueberry muffins from the bakery between his apartment and her place are always so good but they're way too heavy. The croissant is good but it's never enough. "Can we split both?" she asks.

Jeff beams at her. "You're a damn genius. Get a knife."

Sonia does just that, choosing a steak knife from the drawer in case a butter knife isn't strong enough. She brings it to him and watches him cut the two pastries in perfect halves. Then she returns the knife to the sink and comes back to join Jeff at the table. He's already missing two bites of his pumpkin donut. "So what was up with you yesterday?" he asks.

"Just had a fever and a headache. Nothing too serious. Seems to be gone today," she admits.

Jeff nods. "I figured it couldn't be too bad or you would've given me a heads up."

Sonia feels a pang of guilt. Was she supposed to let him know? Technically Jeff is her best, and probably only, friend. When she was hired by her company about two years ago she was surprised to find him working there. She remembered him from high school, of course, but hadn't kept up with what he was doing in his daily life. Some of the girls from work are convinced that Jeff is always hanging around because he wants a relationship with Sonia, but he's never hinted at that or tried anything. They're just really good friends. She wouldn't have it any other way. So does all that mean that Jeff deserves a text when she's out sick even though they're in different departments? Yeah, probably. She sighs. "Shit, I'm sorry. I texted Mark and then went back to bed, honestly. I didn't think about it. I should've sent a text to you too. You probably got asked about it all day."

"Yeah, but it's fine." He smiles in a way that looks forced. "I'm glad you're feeling better."

Sonia takes another sip of her mocha and follows it up with a huge bite of the chocolate donut.

"I'm one hundred percent better after this breakfast of champions," she says.

Jeff laughs. "I can't imagine this is doctor-recommended. Are you planning on working today?" he says, widening his eyes at her outfit. "I'm not criticizing or anything but I think that might be against the company dress code."

Sonia pulls out a leg clad in the pajama bottoms she wore all day yesterday while she was holed up in bed. She wiggles her foot, showing off her pink fuzzy slippers. "You don't think flannel is allowed?"

"At our strict company with its collared shirts rule? No, I can't imagine it is." Jeff jokes.

"I'll get ready quickly. It never takes me long to throw something on. We're carpooling, right?"

"It was already on my schedule." Jeff shoves the last bite of his pumpkin donut in his mouth and picks up his half of the blueberry muffin. "You get dressed. I'll sit here and eat. Then I'll drive and you can finish your pastries in the car."

Sonia stands, shoving the last of her chocolate donut in her mouth. "Deal."

She spins and takes off toward her bedroom as Jeff calls, "Talking with a full mouth is gross."

She laughs. "Don't start with me," she calls. "We don't have time."

"Fine, you're a perfect lady."

She can hear his laughter even as she kicks her bedroom door shut. "It's not that funny," she yells. "I'm mostly a perfect lady."

If she was timing herself, she'd know it takes her twelve minutes to get ready. Jeff was right about the company dress code being pretty strict. She doesn't have many appropriate outfits to choose from but they're never used for anything other than work, meaning there's always enough of them to last her the week. She throws on a clean collared shirt and dress pants. Then she slips her feet into shoes on her way to the bathroom where she spends more than half of her allotted getting ready time. She runs a brush through her hair and throws it in a quick braid, securing it with an elastic. Then she brushes her teeth, washes her face with a disposable wipe, and swipes deodorant under each arm. She read somewhere that she should be using the deodorant at night time after her showers, but she can't quite get in the habit. Lastly, she collects all her electronics and flings open the bedroom door to reenter the dining area of her little condo. "Done," she calls. "How'd I do?"

Jeff pulls up his left sleeve and checks his watch. "We're not late," he says. "We should be just fine unless we get stuck behind a train."

"Then we're safe because what are the odds of that happening twice in one week?" Sonia teases, referencing the train they were stuck behind on Monday morning.

"You just jinxed it," Jeff whines. "Grab your breakfast, we have to jet."

1997

Sonia holds the curling iron far enough away from her face to avoid burning her ear and tries to count in her head like Jeanne told her to. She doesn't want to mumble the numbers out loud because Jeanne always has a comment about that. When she thinks it's been long enough, she slowly lets the curl out and frowns as it stays entirely too tight. She can never quite get this curling thing right.

Jeanne reaches over and runs her fingers through the few curls Sonia has managed, letting them drop a little into something closer to what Jeanne has achieved on her own head. "First day of Junior year," Jeanne says. "Are you excited?"

Sonia shrugs. "I guess." In reality, she always gets nervous before the first day of school. She couldn't sleep last night so she's exhausted and nauseated this morning. But Jeanne doesn't want to hear about that.

"What cute boys do we think will be back?" Jeanne asks. "You think we'll see Tom?" Her voice immediately changes into something higher-pitched when she says Tom.

Sonia shakes her head violently. "No way am I letting you talk me into anything like that again," she says, remembering the embarrassing exchange last year that all started because she let Jeanne talk her into putting a note on his desk before their math class. "I am not doing that again."

"Oh come on, he thought it was cute. I heard that he asked a bunch of people about it, trying to figure out if anyone saw who left the note."

Sonia rolls her eyes and focuses her attention on the next section to curl, the last one to frame her face. "I hope no one told him anything."

"He thought it was cute. He's curious. Isn't that a good thing?"

"No, it's a very bad thing. You're forgetting that I flat-out told him to his face that I didn't write that note. So it's a done deal. I can't admit that I lied."

Jeanne watches as Sonia lets the last curl down. Then she steps behind her and looks into the mirror as she runs her fingers through everything, making the curls look a bit better than they had before. Then she reaches down and unplugs the curling iron. "I still don't understand why you didn't just own up to it," she says.

"Too late now. I'll never admit it was me and I could never stand there talking to him and pretend it wasn't. That ship has sailed." She stands up and grabs her backpack. "Now we have to go before we are late."

"Fine. But I'm just saying, if Tom comes up to you and tries to talk about it —" Jeanne begins.

Sonia waves her hand. "He won't. He doesn't know I'm alive and it's better that way." She taps Jeanne on the end of her nose. "Stop meddling."

"Not meddling. Got it. Sonia knows what she's doing."

"Exactly." Sonia moves beside her friend and links their elbows together. "Now, tell me about some boy you're hoping shows up at school today."

2024

In the car on Friday, Sonia immediately takes control of the radio dial. Jeff reaches out and playfully slaps her hand. "What are you doing? Don't change my station."

Sonia rolls her eyes at him. "If you didn't listen to old man music I wouldn't have to change anything."

"It's not old man music. It's classical. It's good for your brain and it's been around for hundreds of years."

"It's the absolute worst and it will put me to sleep if you insist on listening to it."

"Whatever. You know I'll let you listen to anything you want but you need to use car etiquette. Always ask the driver."

Sonia pulls her hand away from the radio dial and joins it palm-to-palm with her other hand. "Please, oh please, can I turn on something a little more lively for our ridiculously early drive to work?" she asks in a sugar-sweet voice.

"See, was that so hard?" Jeff relents.

"Thank you." Sonia clicks one of the memory buttons below the stereo and changes to a station that plays music from when they were in high school. "I'm going nostalgic today. Get it, because of the reunion?"

Jeff groans. "Are we seriously going to that? I can't change your mind?"

"Why would we change our minds?" Sonia takes another huge bite of her bagel but chews and swallows it before talking again. "We already paid for tickets. We're going."

"And we're doing this because you feel like you have something to prove about the one that got away?"

Sonia can hear the sarcasm in his voice. They've had this discussion before. Heck, they've had a full-on argument about this before. Jeff thinks it's stupid that Sonia puts so much emphasis on that one event in high school she wishes had gone differently. He thinks she's being ridiculous. The worst part of this discussion is that Sonia doesn't disagree with him. She is being ridiculous. She also can't help it. How do you not look back on something like that and wonder how your life would've been different if you hadn't lied? If she'd had the guts to tell the truth about that one thing, would she be living an entirely different life right now? "Don't you have anything in your life that you wonder about?" she asks, instead of cycling back into the old argument again. "Isn't there a girl in your past that you have regrets about? Someone you wish you could say something to? Even once?"

Jeff falls quiet and serious. Sonia recognizes

the difference between his thinking expression and his I'm-avoiding-this-conversation expression. She drinks her coffee and makes her way through her breakfast while he drives. Finally, he sighs. "Of course I have regrets. Everyone does. I guess the difference is that I don't think that one tiny conversation more than twenty years ago would've changed as much as you think it would have."

"I'm not changing anything," Sonia argues. "I just want to see what's happening with him now. If he's completely miserable or has done absolutely nothing with his life since leaving school, I'll know it was the right call."

"And if he isn't miserable or is highly successful?" Jeff prompts.

Sonia thinks. It isn't that she wishes misery on Tom. That's not right. It's that she needs to show herself that she didn't make a huge mistake all those years ago by not telling him the truth. She wants him to be an asshole of, like, epic proportions. Is that so hard to understand? "I think I mean I want him to be someone I wouldn't be happy with. Like, I want to see that being alone in my current life is better than what I would be if I had given something else a chance. Does that make sense?"

Jeff shrugs. "I don't know, I guess. So you want to see that he's not the guy for you. You need this stupid night to prove that to you. Sonia, that's sad.

You see how sad this is, right?"

Sonia rips off a piece of her bagel and lobs it across his car at him. "I'm not sad. Take that back."

Jeff laughs. "Alright, fine. We'll go to the stupid 25-year reunion, which I will go on record as saying is a stupid milestone to even have a reunion for. We'll dance to this music you're playing right now, which is a great blast from the past, and then we'll leave. In the car on the way home, you can tell me 'I told you so' because I'm betting this guy is going to be completely pompous, like he always was, and you'll be so glad you didn't even attempt to pursue anything with him." He holds his hand out toward her without taking his eyes off the road. "Deal?"

Sonia laughs and shakes his hand. "Deal."

1998

"Tell me again what number he is," Sonia says, speaking loud enough to be heard over the roaring fans in the gym full of screaming basketball fans.

Jeanne points. "28, right there."

Sonia nods at the sweaty kid wearing the 28 jersey. She sort of recognizes him. If you subtract the wet hair and the sweat stains marking his dark purple school jersey, that is. "I think I had a class with your new boy toy once Sophomore year," she says.

"Probably. You're in all those advanced classes and he is too. I told you he's not just athletic. He's also cute and smart. I'm so lucky."

"I'm not insulting you," Sonia starts, "but if you were a cartoon character you'd have giant pink hearts for eyes right now and cherubs would be circling your head."

Jeanne laughs and gently punches Sonia in the leg. "Stop teasing. He's cute, right?"

Sonia looks again because to not look would be rude. You can't answer that question without looking. Jeanne wants an honest opinion, not an off-the-cuff answer. She watches the kid run down the court after the guy with the ball. She has no idea what any moves in basketball are called, even if she does know the general point. It doesn't matter. She's not watching to see if he's good at this sport or in the right position. She's watching the athleticism. He has no trouble keeping up with everyone else; he's trim in the right places, and he's a good height. "Yeah, he's cute," she tells Jeanne. "Totally cute."

Jeanne beams. "I know."

Sonia squeezes her best friend's knee. "I'm glad you're happy." Then, to avoid the sappy moment, she focuses back on the court. They're changing lines. At least she thinks that's what's happening. Two guys are kneeling in front of the table where the scorekeeper sits, waiting for their chance to go in. As she watches, the guys stand up and jog into the game. Tom jogs off of the court. He looks up into the stands and Sonia swears their eyes catch. He nods once and then raises his hand in a wave.

"Holy shit," she whispers.

"Did he just wave at you?" Jeanna hisses. "You better wave back."

Before she can think too much about it, Sonia's arm shoots up and she moves it back and forth. It's a small motion, but it's clearly a wave. Her face instantly reddens. "Oh my God, who's behind me?" She turns and looks but there's no one there that looks familiar. "Do you think he was waving at someone else?" she asks Jeanne, her voice frantic.

"It looked like he was waving at you." Jeanne shrugs.

"I'm so embarrassed," Sonia wails. "He was probably waving at someone else and I just looked like a total idiot waving back."

"If he wasn't waving at you then he wasn't looking at you so he didn't see you wave."

"He didn't see me move my arm around in the air?" Sonia asks, skeptically. She repeats the motion. "Everyone sees this."

"Right, and you're doing it right now for no reason. Relax, if he wasn't waving at you he probably didn't even see it."

Sonia relaxes. "Good. You're right. No big deal."

"No big deal," Jeanne echoes. "Except he was waving at you and you do obviously still like him or it wouldn't have just been an issue." She holds her hands up defensively. "Just saying."

Sonia rolls her eyes. "Whatever."

After the game, Sonia stands on the sidewalk outside the gymnasium waiting for her ride. As always, Jeanne's parents were right on time. In fact, it feels like everyone else's parents were right on Tim so Sonia is left standing alone. The parking lot has gotten shockingly empty as she stands here in the dark. She wonders if the gates are open to the campus and the pay phones so she can call and check on her Dad. Maybe he forgot about picking her up?

The door to the gym behind her opens and someone comes out in a blast of laughter. She turns toward the sound and sees Tom stepping out. Quickly she looks away, a flame of heat rushing to her cheeks. "Hey Sonia, how are you?" Tom asks.

Holy shit. Tom knows her name? She scrabbles for her voice. "Good," she squeaks.

"How'd you like the game?" he asks, tipping his head back toward the gym.

"Yeah, it was good. Nice game. You play good." She wants to smack herself on the forehead but resists. She sounds like an idiot.

"Thanks." He adjusts a bag on his shoulder and takes another step closer to the curb and Sonia. "So, what's new?" he asks. "Anything interesting?"

"Um, no. I don't think so." She can't think of anything Tom would've known about her the last time they talked. "How about with you?"

He shrugs. "Yeah, same as always." He shuffles his feet, maybe trying to get warm. "So are you going to the Winter Wonderland dance thing?" He shuffles again. "That's in this same gym," he adds almost as if that's the reason he asked.

Sonia feels like her heart might beat right out of her chest. Is he asking just to be nice and make conversation? Because this feels like it could, possibly, be one of those important moments in life that you can't get back.

Her Dad picks that exact moment to take the right-hand turn into the school parking lot. Sonia figures she has about fifteen seconds to figure out what this means. "Um, yeah. I mean, I'm going with a friend. Jeff, I think you know him. He's had some of the same classes as us before. He's a super nice guy. We figured we should just go together so neither of us has to go alone. Why, are you going?" She stops herself before she can vomit more words at him. That was enough of an answer. Her Dad turns up the aisle, heading right for them.

"I'll probably do the same. Go with friends, I mean."

And Dad's here. Pulling right up in front of her and reaching across to unlock the passenger door. Her Dad with his impeccable timing. "That's my ride," Sonia says.

"I figured. Thanks for coming to the game," Tom says. "I'll see you around."

"Yeah, see you around." In the car, her thoughts spiral. Did that just mean more than casual conversation? Was he asking to be polite or for a reason? She sighs and leans her head on the window. She just did that all wrong, didn't she?

2024

Sonia reluctantly gets off the couch and drags herself to the bedroom to change into something for the reunion. She slips into a shirt that she never wears. One that flatters her in all the right places. Then she pulls on a pair of black slacks that still have a tag because since she bought them, she has yet to find the right place to wear them. A reunion will have to be the place, she decides. She steps into a pair of comfortable shoes she's capable of walking in. It wouldn't do to fall in a pair of high heels in front of everyone she went to high school with. Then she heads to the bathroom where she washes her face clean of the day and proceeds to put on just a touch of understated makeup. She tries to find a good balance between "I look like this all the time, even without makeup" and "Of course I put in effort to see all of you again". She's still trying to decide if she got the balance right when her phone vibrates on the countertop beside her.

Jeff is calling with a video. That's never a good sign. She hits accept but continues to leave him pointed at the ceiling. "What's up?" she asks.

"Don't hate me," he says instead of a proper greeting.

"Not even possible," she tells him. "What's up?"

"I'm not going to be out of here on time after all," he admits, sounding a little sheepish. Jeff had dropped her off after work and headed to get his oil changed, a process that was supposed to take about forty-five minutes. That was closer to two hours ago now. He should already have been on the way to get her.

Sonia picks the phone up off the counter and points it at her face. Now she can see that Jeff is still inside the lobby of the dealership where he took the car. He looks frustrated and tired. "So are we skipping the reunion?" she asks. She has to admit the idea is starting to gain merit. She could just stay home tonight, put her feet up, and have a glass of wine.

"No. We're going. We said we would go and we're going," Jeff insists. "I just can't get out of here and across town in time. They said they were almost done with my car. I don't know what's taking them so long. But I can meet you there if you grab a rideshare."

Sonia hates rideshares but it's not Jeff's fault she also hates driving. If she has the opportunity to be a passenger princess, she will always take it. "I could just bring my car," she starts.

Jeff is already shaking his head. "I can still bring you home. Honest. I'm not going to leave you hanging, I promise. Just order a car and meet me there. Please."

Sonia sighs. "Fine, but only because I've already got just the right amount of makeup on." She pauses to let him slip in a compliment.

"It's perfect." He's so dependable, never misses an opportunity she sets him up for.

Sonia smiles. "Thank you. Text me when you're actually in your car. Then I'll head that way."

Jeff looks up over the top of the screen at something. "I think she's coming my way now. I bet I'm getting my car back any second."

"Text me anyway, I don't want to be there before you."

"Yeah, totally." But she can tell by the way his focus has completely shifted to someone in front of him that he's not listening. The phone starts to drop away from his face a little.

Sonia saves him from having to pretend to listen to her and disconnects the call, setting her phone back on the counter. She'll wait five minutes and then order a car. That's enough time to pour herself a tiny glass of wine to give her a bit of encouragement to get this evening over with.

Eight minutes and one glass of wine later, Sonia climbs into the back of the car she was sent a picture and description of. She quickly sends the information to Jeff with the message "If I go missing, this is the car I was last in".

"Good evening," the driver, Matt—according to his profile in the rideshare app—greets her. Sonia appreciates that he doesn't ask her any other questions before pulling away from the curb.

"Hi," Sonia says. She keeps her eyes on the scenery, mentally making sure the route is the right one.

"Where are you headed tonight, if you don't mind my asking."

"A high school reunion."

"That sounds fun."

Sonia rolls her eyes. "Not really. I mean, I thought so at first too but the more I think about it the more I realize I don't think I want to go. But I promised my best friend, who I also went to high school with, that we could go. The funny part is I actually had to talk him into going in the first place and now we've switched roles, I guess. I'm just nervous."

"That's normal, I think," friendly Matt consoles her. "You haven't seen most of these people in some time. I'm sure it will be fine."

"You're trying to be positive. Think about high school. It wasn't always good. Why do we need to see these people again? I mean, really, what was I thinking?"

"You were thinking it would be good for nostalgic purposes, I'm sure. Most people are usually focused on that."

"I guess," Sonia sighs. "But don't you have that one person in your life you wonder about? The one that you look back on and think about how things might have gone? That person was in high school for me." She shakes her head, wondering why she's sharing all this with a stranger. She tries to get herself to stop talking. But something is bubbling up inside of her trying to get out. "I don't know why I'm thinking about him so much this week. It's strange, really. I haven't thought about him in decades and now my mind keeps coming back to him and that darn note."

"Note?" Matt inquires.

Sonia waves her hand. "It's nothing." She doesn't know why she can't stop thinking about it if it's nothing. "Nothing," she repeats. She has to stop going down this rabbit hole. Where is all of this coming from?

"You wonder what might have been different?" Matt says. His voice sounds almost reverent.

Sonia risks a look at him. She can only see his profile, but he's smiling. "Yeah, sometimes. I guess."

The front of the car makes a strange noise. Not a noise that should be concerning. More like the sound from a video game or maybe a notification for an app. Except that it came from the car, not from a phone. At least it sounded like it was coming from the car. "What was that?" Sonia asks.

Matt reaches out and smacks the center console. "Oh, just something starting. Nothing to worry about at all."

The car pulls to a stop at a curb. Sonia looks out the window and is startled to see they've arrived. She would've guessed they had a few more minutes. "Oh, you made good time," she says.

"I try. You be safe out there."

"Right. Thanks." She opens the door and steps out into the cool night air, pulling her sweater tighter around her.

"Enjoy the walk into things," Matt says just as she's closing the door.

Sonia shivers a little. That was a strange ride. She turns and faces the tall and imposing building. It has large doors and no windows that she can see. The address is posted in huge numbers just to the right of the doors. Sonia checks it against the address she was given, verifying that this is the right place. There's no signage for the reunion, no people milling around. She has the strangest feeling she might be in the wrong place but everything appears valid.

She pulls open the heavy exterior door and steps inside. In front of her a hallway seems to stretch out forever. There are sconces evenly spaced along both walls, providing circles of light along the otherwise empty hallway. She hears no noise, sees no people or doors.

This is probably a stupid idea, she decides, as she starts to walk down the hallway.

Minutes pass and nothing changes. She feels no further along the hallway, although she keeps taking measured steps. Spinning around, she looks back in the direction she came. Her heartbeat hammers in her chest. Behind her, the view matches that in front of her. No doorways, no people. But she came in that way. She's sure of it. Panic begins to swell, hot and prickly. She picks up the pace, having the terrible feeling she's going in the wrong direction but everything looks the same. How can you go in the wrong direction when you aren't sure what the right direction is?

Just as she feels like she might drop to the floor and have a good breakdown, she catches sight of a door ahead of her.

She's not ashamed to admit that she runs to that door. There's a part of her that is terrified the door will never draw closer, that she will just watch it remain there and never actually close the distance. But that doesn't happen. She reaches it and pushes the door open.

1996

Sonia holds the paperback in front of her face, pretending to be completely engrossed. She hopes no one can see her embarrassed flush, which she's sure is covering her entire neck and face. She's also hoping this makes her look so busy that no one will interrupt her. This entire experiment was a huge mistake. She can't believe she let Jeanne talk her into it. She wishes she could take it all back, but it's too late now. There are too many people in the classroom. When she dropped the paper, it was just her and the math teacher. Even the teacher, after giving her the perfunctory head nod, turned his back to her to write on the board. She's pretty sure he didn't care about the paper she dropped on a desk. But if she got up now everyone in this third-period class would see her retrieve it. She has no choice; she has to leave it.

She reads the first paragraph on this page again, attempting to focus on fictional worlds. The chatter at the door gets louder, the signal that someone new and cool is approaching the classroom. Sonia lowers her head even further, hiding behind the paperback. "Oh my God, I thought you were going to be absent or something," she hears. This voice belongs to Amanda. The most adorable girl ever to exist. If Amanda and Sonia were standing side-by-side no boy in their right mind would pay any attention to Sonia. At least, so far they haven't.

"Have I ever missed a day of this class?" Tom asks. Sonia, who would've thought her neck was already as low as it could go, drops her head further. She cannot believe she let Jeanne talk her into this. It was a really stupid plan.

Tom takes a second in the doorway to scan the room. His second-period class is on the other side of the school so he's usually the last person to make it to this class on time. It looks like today is no different. All twenty of the people he is used to sitting near for this advanced course are accounted for. A few are standing by the door. These kids are like flies. They hang out near whomever they think is the best for their social status at all times. They're nice enough and will boost your ego, but they have no real personality. He wonders if they even continue to exist when no one else is around, maybe they fade into the background like ghosts.

His eyes land on the desk he always sits in. Left half of the room but on the inner aisle. He says it's so he can stretch out his long legs, which he does, but it's really because that puts him center of the classroom and perfectly in front of the board. He plays his cool guy persona well at school, even when that means hiding what a good student he is.

Today, there's a small square of paper sitting

on his desk. He squints and moves closer. Probably the paper was left by whoever sat there during second period. That happens all the time. It could be stray notes from their own class. It could be a stupid note that says "Hi, I sit here too." Or, it could be something juicier. Something dropped by accident that was not meant for his eyes. Something that gives him a little gossip he can use to his advantage. Everyone likes gossip. If he can feed the flies with someone new, they stop paying attention to every little detail of his life for a few days.

No such luck, he muses. The note on the desk has his name printed in light letters, perfectly spaced and even height. Someone who has near-perfect penmanship left him a note.

The bell rings. Mr. Zucker pushes himself up from behind his desk and waves his hand. "That's the bell. Take your seats." Tom drops into his chair and pulls a notebook out of his backpack. He opens the notebook to a blank page, spreads his single sheet of looseleaf with the homework problems over the top, and leaves the little note with his name visible underneath the pile. He plans to wait for a good moment to open it. Right now, during homework check time, too much attention is on the students. He wouldn't get away with it.

Zucker's voice gets louder. "I said take your seats." Tom looks up to see Amanda and a few of the other flies still standing. They're close to their usual seats, but they're taking their time. He wonders if they have seen the note and decides they likely have. That's why they were all waiting for him by the door. It's why they're moving slowly now. They're all waiting to see what he does with it. He pulls on the note just a little, so it's sticking out from below the notebook. He's hoping he communicated that he intends to wait to read it. They may as well sit.

As if cued by a conductor, they all drop into their chairs. Tom shakes his head. "Let's get started. Last night you were assigned twelve problems. We can go over as many as four right here on the board together. Who would like to see a problem worked out?" Zucker booms.

Amanda's hand flies up. "I'd like to see number seven, please."

There are groans from the class. The answers to the odd-numbered problems are in the back of the textbook. For that reason, the students know to only ask to see even numbered problems. This maximizes the number of answers you are sure are correct. Tom glances down at his paper. He did number seven and got the answer at the back.

While Zucker turns his attention to the board, showing the steps for solving the problem, Tom slips the paper out from underneath the notebook and into his lap. He carefully unfolds the paper, trying not to let it rustle. Inside, the handwriting is the same as the front. Light pencil marks are perfectly spaced and form uniform letters. No loopy cursive, no hearts over any letters. Just simple handwriting.

He squints a little at the light lettering.

> *Tom,*
> *First, this was not my idea. I was perfectly fine with you going through our entire sophomore year without ever knowing this information. But, I've been talked into telling you. I think you're cute and I have a crush on you. I would bet money that you hear that all the time. Basketball fans must flock to you daily, gushing about how amazing you are. I'm sure it doesn't mean anything that some anonymous girl wants to tell you … again. But here's the thing, I have never seen a basketball game. I don't think you're cute because of how you play. I like the way you look when you are talking about Shakespeare in English. I like the way you look when you're laughing with your friends at lunch. Anyway, enough embarrassing stuff. I just wanted you to know that someone sees the real you … and likes what they see. Have a nice day.*

It's not signed. Tom looks up at the front of the room and sees that Zucker has moved on to solving number 10. He glances down at his homework paper and realizes he stopped solving that problem halfway through. Shit. He quickly shoves the note under his notebook again and focuses on the teacher. He copies the new steps and carefully boxes the answer he can't believe he didn't get on his own.

"Alright, enough free answers," Zucker booms in that loud voice only he can get away with using in the classroom. "Take out your notes."

Tom passes his homework sheet forward. Then he leans to his left. "Hey, did you see who dropped this?" he whispers to the kid beside him. This kid's name is Jeff, Tom knows. He is ridiculously smart and thinks he is invisible. He listens to great music choices and could be a great addition to the soccer team if he liked sports. He's the kind of guy Tom imagines he would be friends with in another reality. One where he's allowed to be who he wants to be instead of who he's supposed to be. Jeff nods and points toward the front of the room to a girl with a long ponytail and terrible posture. She looks like she is trying to sink into the little plastic chair underneath her. "Thanks," Tom whispers before straightening back up.

He spends the rest of the class period taking careful notes, trying not to think about the letter, paying attention to the teacher as best as he can, and trying not to sneak peeks at the girl who dropped the letter. He knows her name is Sonia. He knows she shares five of the classes on his schedule. She definitely isn't one of the flies, which is pretty obvious from her letter and her behavior. She doesn't seem to care what anyone thinks of her. Honestly, before today he hadn't given her a second thought. Now he can't seem to stop thinking about her long enough to pay attention to the math notes he is supposed to be writing.

The bell rings and Tom scrambles to stuff the notebook back in his bag. Usually, he's packed and ready before that bell rings. He can't believe he was sitting here daydreaming. He rushes out of the door, the note in his clenched fist. She's at least three people ahead of him, walking in the same direction he needs to go. He rushes. "Sonia," he calls. "Hang on, wait a second."

Sonia stops and looks over her shoulder, her eyes creased in confusion. When she spots him, a blush takes over her entire face. She whips back around and continues walking. "Wait, hang on a second," he calls.

When she pulls to the left and steps out of the flow of traffic under an overhang, he hurries to catch up. He pulls the note out of his back pocket. "I wanted to ask you about this," he says. He's surprised to find his embarrassment is strong. What if it was a joke? What if she didn't mean any of it? It does seem odd that she would know exactly what he was thinking. "Is this, maybe, from you?" he asks.

Sonia looks down at the paper in his hand and mumbles something, but he can't understand her.

"What?" he asks. "I'm not mad if that's what

you're worried about. It's just really flattering. I'd like to find whoever wrote it."

Her blush deepens and she nods, slowly. The gesture is small as if daring him to ignore it or pretend not to see it. Instead, he smiles. "This is so flattering," he repeats. "I didn't know you felt that way. I didn't even know you knew who I was."

"Everyone knows who you are," Sonia says quietly.

"Not like this," Tom says. "You seem to know me. Like, the real me. Do you think I could, maybe, get your phone number so I can call you sometime?"

Sonia pulls her backpack around to the front of her body and slips a pen out of the small pocket in the front. She uses it to scribble seven digits onto the bottom of the note. "You can call me," she says, "I'd like that."

"I will," Tom says. "Count on it."

2024

The door moves when Sonia pushes it and opens into a bright room full of people. She breathes a sigh of relief. "Sonia, wait up," a voice calls from behind her. She turns and sees what is clearly an older version of Tom hustling toward her. He's sporting new lines around his eyes, his face is generally wider, and he's as unlikely as she is to fit into the pants size he would've worn in high school, but it's unmistakably him.

Sonia takes a step to the side, assuming he'll hustle past her and into the reunion. Instead, he pulls to a stop directly in front of her. "We agreed to walk in together, remember?" he says. "We have to keep up appearances."

Sonia feels like she's underwater. "What?"

"Don't be a bitch, Sonia. I'm not asking you to go home with me when it's over. I'm just asking you to put on appearances while we're here. Just pretend to be happy like you used to. That's all I'm asking." He reaches up and runs his fingers through his hair in a gesture that instantly takes Sonia back to watching him in high school in a way she never thought anything could. What is happening?

"I promise after tonight we'll deal with the public breakup," Tom continues. "Now is not the time."

Sonia has absolutely no idea what to say to this. She has no idea what the hell he's talking about. She opens her mouth, planning to ask. But he spins on his heel and takes a step toward the noise and the lights. Sonia sort of drifts after him, completely confused. He reaches back and takes her hand. Tom is holding her hand. At the reunion. What the hell is happening?

Sonia lets him lead her around the floor while she tries to think. She got in that car and the rideshare guy drove her here. The hallway, that was weird. Is she dreaming? Could she have fallen asleep in that car? Maybe she was drugged. Maybe this isn't real. Maybe this is her brain's way of coping with how stressed she was about the reunion. That must be it. This is a dream. She's dreaming about what life might have been like if she had been with Tom, chosen Tom.

Tom stops walking and Sonia stands beside him. He's led them to a group of six or seven faces Sonia vaguely remembers. He drapes his arm over her shoulder and talks to the group. Sonia sort of filters in and out of the conversation, the way one would in a dream. They talk about nothing. Sonia gets the sense that Tom is some kind of minor celebrity in this dream world. She tries to remember if she thought of him that way before. Has she ever checked to see what he is up to in the real world now? She can't remember ever doing that. She wonders if this version of her in the dream thinks things are different now for both of them. Maybe her dream self is merely filling in details real Sonia hasn't bothered to research.

"Have you two been together this entire time?" one of the girls asks. She sort of scowls at Sonia as if to say she doesn't belong there, under Tom's arm. Sonia resists the urge to tell the girl that she is personally more shocked than anyone else about this turn of events.

"Ever since Sonia wrote me the cutest love note," Tom says. He looks at her with an expression that makes her stomach flip-flop in the best way. "She was the first person who ever saw the real me," he says.

What the hell? Sonia remembers that day, obviously. She wrote a note because Jeanne told her to. She left it on his desk. He read it. He asked her about it.

The memory slams into her. He asked her about it, she remembers that. But suddenly she can remember it two ways. She can remember saying she didn't write it but she can also, just as clearly, remember saying she did. She remembers writing her phone number on the note. She remembers telling him to call her.

Sonia feels sick. "I think I need to use the

restroom," she says suddenly. "Anyone know where it is?" One of the girls points toward one wall and Sonia nods. "Perfect. I'll just be right back."

She maneuvers out from under Tom's arm and heads in the direction the girl pointed She's finding it hard to catch her breath. Something about this feels decidedly un-dreamlike. She turns into the opening labeled restrooms and finds an empty hallway. She leans against the wall and takes two deep breaths. There, in the quiet of the hallway, she lets herself consider the strangest possibility.

What if this is an alternate reality? One where she chose differently. One where that second memory is true.

How could she test that? How could she create a test that would let her prove or disprove the dream theory? She thinks of the obvious one first. Pinch yourself, isn't that what everyone says? In a dream, it wouldn't hurt. She makes the pinching motion and closes her grip around her forearm, hard. It hurts. She stops. Well, that's not exactly concrete, she supposes. But it's a vote in favor of this not being a dream. What else behaves differently in a dream, besides pain? People, she realizes. People behave differently. In a dream, people just sort of act the way you expect them to act. Where, in reality, people will call out strange behaviors. She'll find someone, behave strangely, and see what happens.

Sonia makes her way back out into the crowded room. She intentionally crashes into someone nearby, a lady in a green blouse whom Sonia doesn't recognize at all. The girl turns around quickly. "Oh, what the hell," she says. "Watch where you're going. I almost spilled my drink."

Typical reaction, Sonia thinks. That didn't help. She considers stepping on this girl's toe, just to see what she would do. Push that boundary.

"Oh my God, you're Sonia."

"Um, yeah. Do I know you?" Sonia asks. A half second later she remembers where she is. "Did we have a class together in high school or something?"

"No, my husband went to school with you." The girl waves her hand like that fact is inconsequential. "But I follow you on social media. Your life is kind of amazing. I'm a huge fan. Can I get a selfie with you?"

Sonia has absolutely no idea what to say to this. She wants to ask which social media platform, specifically. She has a lot of them but rarely posts on any of them. She wants to tell this poor girl she has the wrong person. Except, the girl had her name and knew what high school she went to. Plus, presumably, Sonia's picture would accompany any social media. She settles for allowing the girl to take a quick selfie, which she's sure she looks positively awkward for, and then excuses herself right back to that quiet hallway.

When she's alone again, she pulls out her cell phone and opens one of the many social media apps she has but never uses. She clicks the profile button on the bottom of the screen to see her recent posts, expecting to see the sad mostly blank boxes of someone who never posts. Instead, her screen fills with perfectly curated little pictures of a life Sonia does not remember living. There are shots of her posing in front of places Sonia has never been. Shots of her and Tom with their arms around each other, smiling. Shots of a house she has never seen before. Even some of a cute golden retriever she certainly doesn't own. The top of the page shows a handle that is something she would use and the picture of the profile is definitely, unmistakably her.

Her eyes track to the right, to a follower count. She almost drops her phone in shock. There are over two million people following this account for a girl who looks exactly like Sonia and who has logged in on Sonia's own phone but lives a life Sonia knows nothing about.

"Jesus, can't you leave that shit behind for one night?"

Sonia looks up from her phone to find Tom scowling at her. "What?" she says, taken aback by the hostility when he was so kind in front of all those people a minute before.

"Your followers don't need you posting at our fucking reunion. Just be present for one night." He shakes his head. "Actually, do whatever the hell you want. Just don't take pictures of me tonight. You agreed." He pushes open the nearby door labeled as the men's room without giving her a chance to respond.

Sonia can't possibly understand what is happening. This is not something her mind would've concocted. It's far beyond what she can imagine and it has entirely too many moving parts. So, apparently, she has found herself in some kind of alternate reality where she's with Tom but unhappy about it. But her social media, which is full of people following what seems to be a perfect life, shows none of that unhappiness. Plus, in this reality, Tom is talking about a break-up they will need to announce.

Sonia is not sure she likes this new life. That leaves one very important question, how does she get back to her own reality?

2024

Sonia walks out of the hallway and back into the room full of people who know her as someone else entirely. She stands there, wondering what to do. Should she open her rideshare app and try to find that driver? Should she just leave the building and see if she can find her way back to that weird hallway?

Her eyes catch on someone. They're by the front of the room where a dance floor has been erected. It takes a few beats of staring before her brain catches up with what she's seeing. Jeff is here.

Of course that makes sense, since he did go to high school with her in both universes, presumably. She feels the sudden urge to talk to him like she would in her universe. Almost as if she expects he would solve everything if only she gave him the chance.

She crosses the room in a few quick strides and suddenly she's in front of him. "Hello," he says. It's not the warm greeting she wanted. It's more hesitant like he's trying to place her. That hesitation breaks her heart. Jeff is the most steady, reliable part of the reality she remembers. He's the one person she can always count on. To think that this is a world where he isn't that, where she doesn't have that, hurts.

"Hi. I don't know if you remember me. You're Jeff, right?" She swallows and tries to think of how high school Sonia would've approached this. "I think we had some classes together in Sophomore and Junior years. I'm Sonia."

"Oh, yeah, of course. How have you been?" He reaches out and snags the elbow of a cute little blond next to him. She turns her face toward him and Sonia catches the beautiful full smile of someone enamored with Jeff's charm. "Elizabeth, this is Sonia. We were great friends in high school. Sonia, this is my wife Elizabeth."

Wife. It slams into her chest like a punch. In this reality, Jeff is married to this adorable pixie of a woman who smiles at him adoringly in public. "Hi, it's so great to meet you." Elizabeth holds out her hand and Sonia shakes it. "I've heard stories about you before. You sound like a fun person. What are you up to now?" she pushes.

Sonia has no idea how to answer this question. What does the Sonia of this reality do for a living? Presumably, she doesn't work with Jeff, since he didn't recognize her right away. She tries to think of her social media page and what that taught her. She's the kind of person who obsesses over her followers if Tom's reaction is any indication. She has a dog, probably. And a house that looks too large for her.

"She's an influencer, I think," Jeff answers. "Did I see that right? You're with Tom." He looks to Elizabeth, "The one from that action movie we saw last year."

Action movie. Sonia blinks in surprise. She got the impression Tom was someone important from piecing together the clues earlier but she didn't figure him for an action movie star. Somehow that feels shocking. But she doesn't know enough about her own life to disagree. "Yeah, that's right. What are you up to now?" she deflects to take some of the heat off of herself.

"I work in advertising," Jeff says. His entire face lights up with this information like it truly brings him joy. Sonia didn't know he had any interest in advertising. He's never mentioned it. How is it possible that this Jeff, who she doesn't even recognize, is so much happier than her version?

Elizabeth hits him playfully on the chest. "Don't be modest. He owns his own advertising firm and he's partnering to start a new e-zine next year."

"E-zine?" Sonia questions.

"A magazine but digital, delivered to your devices. It's going to focus on creative writing and books, sort of a passion project for both of us." Elizabeth shrugs. "I'm a writer."

"So you married a beautiful writer, started a successful business in advertising, and are now branching out into a magazine passion project," Sonia summarizes. Literally, none of those details are things she would've guessed Jeff wanted out of life. And yet here he is, positively beaming with a happiness she has never seen before.

"That about sums it up," Jeff says with a little laugh. "It's not 1.3 million followers on social media and married to a movie star, but we like it."

"2 million," Sonia says. It's a knee-jerk reaction and she has no idea where it came from. Is she the kind of person who normally corrects this sort of thing? She wouldn't have thought so but something about it feels so right.

"Wow, that's impressive," Elizabeth says. "We should probably step out for a second and make that phone call," she says to Jeff. "Check on the baby."

Baby. The bombshells just keep dropping.

"Yeah, we should." He holds out his hand to Sonia. "It was great catching up. We should stay in touch. I'll message you on your socials, yeah? Maybe we can get lunch."

"Yeah, of course. That would be great." She watches them walk away, Jeff's arm around Elizabeth's waist in a way that feels organic and natural instead of the forced way Tom grabbed onto Sonia.

She can't do this anymore. She has no idea what comes next or how to fix this but she can't be here in this room that feels too small and too full of people. She needs to be somewhere where she can breathe.

2024

This time the door to the main room doesn't lead to a long hallway with no doors and no end in sight. Instead, when Sonia pulls the main door open she's already on the walkway where she entered the building. And there, as if he'd been there all along, is the driver who dropped her off.

Sonia opens the back door and drops onto the seat. She didn't call him or request that he come back, but she absolutely doesn't care.

"How was it?" the driver, who Sonia thinks was named Mike, asks.

"Fucking awful," Sonia answers. She's conscious of the fact that she isn't one to curse around strangers normally because she doesn't know how other people feel about it and she doesn't like to offend anyone. She wonders if this is an aspect of her personality that is different in this reality, like automatically correcting someone on her follower count. "Take me home."

Mike turns in his seat, draping his arm over the back so he can properly face her. "And what home would that be?" he asks, entirely too calmly for the situation. "Either is possible. I just need a decision."

Sonia feels like the air has been sucked out of the car. Panic wells in her chest, pooling in her eyes, ready to come down her face as hot tears. "You did this, didn't you?" she asks. Her voice is quiet because the panic is strangling her. "This is real, isn't it? I'm not dreaming? I'm really in some alternate reality and you put me here."

"Parallel universe, actually, and this is the only chance you get, I'm afraid. I'll need that decision. Where are we going back to? Once I put the car in drive the choice is final. Take your time."

Sonia sinks back into the seat. In this reality, she and Tom are clearly miserable. She can't imagine being happy in a life where someone she is supposed to love talks to her with contempt when no one is looking. She doesn't want the pressure of a perfectly cultivated social media presence. None of that sounds like something she would want. She almost sits forward and tells him to take her back home, to her friends and her life.

It's the thought of friends, of Jeff specifically, that keeps her sitting back. Because this isn't just about her. She didn't only change her life. In this life, Tom is an action movie star. Jeff is happily married to a beautiful woman named Elizabeth. They have a child. An actual baby who didn't exist in her other world. A child who gets a chance at a life with happy parents because of a single choice she made twenty-five years ago.

This isn't about her.

Maybe it never was.

Sonia sits forward and smiles to show Mike she's serious. Her panic is already calming with her decision, she's that confident that she's right. "Take me to this home, wherever that is."

Mike's eyes go wide with shock. "My, that's not what I thought you would say." He reaches for the gear selector but stops just shy of touching it. "Are you sure?" he asks.

"I'm sure," she says. "A lot of people are better in this universe. A baby gets a chance every baby should get in this universe. It's better for Jeff if you let me stay here."

"If you insist." The driver turns so he is facing front again. He moves with deliberate slowness as if giving her time to change her mind. She doesn't stop him. He moves the gear shifter down and immediately back up. "We leave it as it is right now," he says. "Good luck, my dear."

Sonia turns her head to look out the window and sees that they are already somewhere new. They're on the curb in front of the house she recognizes from the curated social media feed. Large and imposing, the house looks like it costs a fortune to maintain. Sonia opens the door and peeks into her purse, where she finds a set of keys she doesn't recognize. "Will things start to come back to me or feel more natural?" she asks.

"I'm not sure. I'm just the driver," he answers.

"Thank you. For everything."

Sonia exits the car and watches it drive away. Then she turns to the house and tries one of the keys in the lock. It opens easily. She pushes the door, stepping into a room with a high-vaulted ceiling that feels entirely too large for her. Her phone dings and she holds it up to her face. A text message from Tom reads "Where the hell did you go?"

"Home," she types, "I went home." She realizes she doesn't even know if this is her home, his home, or a shared home. It doesn't matter. This is her life now and she has to get used to it. She opens a nearby door and finds a row of coats hanging. Everything in here is higher end than what she has on. Still, what choice does she have? This is her new normal. She slips out of her coat and adds it to the collection. Then she lets her instinct guide her to the kitchen. She's pleased when she finds it on the first try. In the doorway, she closes her eyes and lets her motor skills go where they want, finding the light switch easily. She opens her eyes to see a beautiful kitchen, impeccably clean. She could have fun trying to learn to cook in a place like this. Do Jeff and Elizabeth have a nice kitchen, she wonders.

Then she almost laughs out loud. In her other life, the other universe, she would sometimes have random thoughts about Tom. She would wonder what he was doing, if he was successful, if he was happy. Now, in this universe, she guesses those thoughts will always be about Jeff.

Perhaps, Sonia thinks, she is destined to be the girl who is never content with her decisions. Always wondering if she did the right thing.

She crosses the kitchen to a large stainless steel refrigerator and pulls open the doors. It's strange how this act feels more like herself than anything else she has done tonight. She wonders if she's getting more comfortable here, or if there is something about eating that will always feel universal. The fridge is full of things Sonia can imagine herself eating. There are healthy options like yogurt, cucumbers, and carrots. But there are also things that aren't exactly on any dietician's meal plan: dark chocolate, full sugar jam, and chocolate pudding. She reaches for a small chocolate bar, unwraps it, and takes a bite.

This is it, Mike told her. No second chances. No third chances either, since technically that's what another chance would be. This decision is final. She owes it to herself to take it seriously and try her best.

She shuts the fridge door and turns, again, to look at her beautiful kitchen. "I can do this," she says quietly to the room. She'll have to. Jeff is happy. A baby has a chance. This, she's confident, was the

right decision.
    It has to be.

Holed Up

A quick story, more of a scene really, this one came from the brainstorming for a bigger story I am still working on drafting. This entire scene centered around one idea: if everything you know changed tomorrow, what could you trust?

As they stand behind the glass wall of windows lining the penthouse, they watch the lights of the city below wink out one by one until the entire scene before them is pitch black and reflects their images. He breathes a resigned sigh. "Electricity failure, as expected." Then he turns away from the windows as if turning his back on that life is as simple an act. His footsteps fade away from her, away from the life they'd known before this. "Good thing we were prepared." His voice is filled with a cheery nature that doesn't at all match what they just witnessed.

She turns to take in what he is seeing. The

lanterns, three burning and fifteen still boxed and stacked against the wall. The cans and boxes of food that won't spoil. The propane bottles lined up near the camping stove they power. The water, cases and cases of it, stretching into the other room of the hotel suite. She lingers on the door, making sure the locks are turned the right way and the security bolt is thrown. Then her eyes find him again. He is watching her, the shake of his head telling her he caught her in the act of rechecking the door. She knows he is judging her for that, not trusting any of this to keep them safe as he has promised. He wants her to trust him but how can she? Neither of them has ever done this before. No one has.

"Hungry?" he asks. "I can make us something."

She shakes her head. She's never hungry anymore. She will eat if he is eating because it seems like she should. But that grumbling in her stomach, the one she used to get, has faded like her will to live. How much time will they have to spend up here? Will there ever be an end? Is the world she remembers ever going to exist again?

"I'm going to heat up some of that beef stew stuff," he says. He crosses to the wall of canned food, crouching down to investigate. He pulls a single can out of the stack, careful to let the others slowly release to keep the pile from falling. He waves it at her. "Found one. It's the good stuff. The brand you like."

She remembers having that brand a few times before. She doesn't remember registering an opinion on the quality. After all, before this, she was the type to make beef stew from fresh ingredients, letting it simmer all day to bring out the flavor. Opening a can used to seem so beneath her. It is ironic now that opening those cans is saving her life. The preservatives she used to try to avoid are now the things allowing her to eat anything at all months after this all started.

She watches him open the can with a manual can opener. They'd taken it from the store they looted when they took the cans. Their electric one wouldn't work forever, he'd claimed. One more thing he was right about. She's lost count of how many things he has been right about since that first day.

She watches him dump the contents of the large, fat can into a saucepan. She wrinkles her nose at the glop it makes. It looks like dog food.

He uses a match to light the burner on the little camping stove and sets the pan over the flame. "Won't be long now," he says. "This baby should heat pretty fast." Again, she notices the cheeriness in his tone. This time she wonders if it is fake or genuine. Maybe he's enjoying this? How is that possible?

He tips his head toward the thing she'd scoffed at him for bringing: the wine rack. Bottles of wine neatly fit into the little metal framework, and a corkscrew hangs from it. It was the only thing he'd dragged into the penthouse that didn't scream "doomsday prepping" and it is completely out of place up here. "Should I open one?" he asks.

She catches herself smiling. Such a simple act but one so unfitting. Perhaps that's why he dragged that thing up here. To give her a quick moment, when things were at their literal darkest out there, to remind her of something normal. Suddenly that's exactly what she wants. A glass of wine with dinner. Something so ordinary. She nods, vehemently. "Pour a big one. Do we have any real glasses?"

The penthouse suite they've barred themselves in is fully furnished. She's sure when they built this high-end place it was a way to be the best, to allow their clients to vacation in style. The manufacturers probably never assumed it would be used to allow someone to stay indoors during what can only be called an apocalypse. To keep a pair of nobodies like them safe from whatever else happens out there while the world falls apart.

He opens a nearby cabinet and digs around. "Aha," he proclaims and he turns to reveal two long stem wine glasses.

They're like a lightning bolt striking her memory. They're exactly the kind of glasses she would've been given at an expensive anniversary-only kind of restaurant before all of this started. They're delightfully fragile in a way most of the items they've accumulated to keep them safe are not. As if existing in this world will shatter them. Her smile widens. "Perfect," she says.

A new energy buzzes through her limbs and she finally moves away from the darkened window and toward him. "I'll stir dinner," she says. It takes her two drawers in the little kitchenette before she finds where he has put the large spoons. By the time she is back at the camping stove, small bubbles have formed in the liquid of the pan. She removes the lid and stirs. Her nose catches the scent and she feels it, that small grumble in her stomach. Perhaps it is not as silent as she thought. Perhaps, no matter what she is thinking, her body still craves those basic things necessary for her survival. It's as if her body is telling her what her brain won't admit.

She does want to live.

Even if living no longer looks the same.

Halloween Party

An original version of this story once appeared as a guest post on a blog. Of course, that was years ago and lots of things have changed. So, I decided to take the story back and give it a much darker ending. On Halloween night, can you even trust your eyes?

I cautiously knock on the door as I mask my disgust at tonight's event under a carefully practiced, although utterly fake, smile. The door flings open, revealing my best friend dressed head-to-toe in black, which I was expecting. Her hair is perfectly curled and flowing lightly around her shoulders, also expected. But the frazzled look on her face complete with wide, darting eyes is shocking, to say the least.

"Christie, I'm so glad you're here." Emily pulls me into the room. "Matt, Christie is here," she bellows over her shoulder. Matt is my oldest brother. He and Emily married this past February. Things between us are still a little weird. How do you adjust to being the third wheel with the two most important people in your life? I haven't figured that out yet.

"It looks great in here." I mean it. The living room of their apartment looks so different under candlelight. Everything is dark and somehow ominous. There are three or four people I recognize seated around the living room. There's an entire table of food that looks better than anything Emily and Matt are capable of whipping up, and a Ouija board is on the coffee table. Everything has a cliche Halloween vibe to it, which I'm sort of digging. This might actually turn out to be fun.

Settling my eyes back on Emily, I'm struck again by how different she looks. Her face is set in this tight mask, but her eyes are crazed. I assumed, when she opened the door, that her frazzled look was in answer to having to throw a Halloween dinner party. Maybe she thought I was someone else at the door and was worried. But it's not fading. If anything, she looks even more scared as we cross her living room. "Emily, are you alright?" I brush her arm to slow her down on her path to the food and speak in a quiet tone. I hope she's not fighting with my brother, that would be an awkward thing to take sides in.

"Of course. I'm fine." She forces a fake smile. "It's just…" she trails off, glancing nervously around the room. "You see them too, right?" Emily jerks her head in the direction of the couch.

I look past her, taking a more careful look at the people I noticed earlier. Chris, from Emily's accounting firm, is in a chair eating what I know is grapes Emily peels and calls eyeballs for this particular holiday. Justin, a guy we grew up with, is seated on the couch next to a woman I'm pretty sure I've seen him with before, whose name I can't recall. One more person is loading up a plate at the food table, but their back is to me. I don't see my brother anywhere. "You mean Chris, Justin, and what's her name?" I ask.

"Yes," Emily hisses. She puts on her fake hostess smile again and speaks loudly for the room. "I'll show you where Matt is, he'll be so glad to see you. Follow me."

This is creepy. I've known Emily for a long time so I can confidently say she's being weird. She grabs my arm and pulls me into the kitchen. Maybe I'll get some answers when we're alone. The door swings shut behind us. My brother is sitting at the kitchen table. His leg is jostling and he keeps running his right hand up through his hair. He stands up. "Oh thank God. Christie, we need you to figure this shit out. I told Em this whole Halloween party was a bad idea."

My heart rate doubles. "What are we talking

about?" I look back and forth between my panicked brother and my best friend. He is not making this better because Matt is never frantic. If Emily is being weird, Matt is being terrifying.

"Emily had this dumb idea to try the seance with just the two of us. We thought it would be fun, right? So we sat down in the living room and got things all ready. We had a few glasses of wine. We tried to summon spirits or something. Those people just kind of showed up." He waves his arm in the direction of the door I came through before using the same hand and pushing his hair back again.

I feel my body matching his nervous energy, a truly bad habit. "What are you talking about? We know those people. They're friends of ours. Emily probably invited them." Still, the hairs on the back of my arms are standing at attention.

"No," Emily jumps in. Her head is shaking side-to-side, sending her careful curls swinging. "You don't get it. They didn't come knocking on the door. They just kind of materialized in the spots they're sitting in." Emily stares daggers at me. "Go see for yourself," she dares.

Well no harm in checking, I suppose. Someone has to be level-headed about this. I grab a bottle of rum and a 2-liter of cola off the counter on my way to the swinging door. I push the door with my hip and re-enter the dark and ominous living room. "Who wants a cocktail?"

I stop, bottles halfway up toward my ears. Chris still has three eyeball things on his plate and one on his fork. He isn't moving. Justin and the girl are still seated on the couch, her leg is frozen in a sort of mid-cross, just hanging in the air in front of her. They are also not moving.

I step closer to the food table to get a better look at this person who still hasn't stepped any nearer to the table or the food it holds. I don't recognize her. She's wearing a long white dress. Her hair is long, straight, and dark. It falls slightly in front of her rather sweet-looking face. She looks younger than us. She is also frozen in place, hand outstretched toward the table.

I back away through the swinging door. "What the hell did you two do?" I whisper. My heart is racing. Something about this is so incredibly wrong.

"Right? How do we fix this?" Matt asks.

"They've just been frozen like that since the seance?" I ask.

"Yes."

"They don't move at all?"

"No," Matt drops his head into his hands. "It's scary, right?"

I push the door open again and step back out. I stand in front of Justin. "Hey, you. How's it going? How's life?"

Nothing.

I wave my hand in front of his face.

Nothing.

I look at Chris. The poor guy hasn't even gotten that grape up to his lips yet. "Well you two are no help, I'm heading back to the kitchen now." I turn to do just that.

She has moved.

I'm pretty sure the girl at the food table has moved. She is at a different angle, I can see her face a little better now. The last time I was out here I had to maneuver myself to see around her hair. I stare at her, a scream rising at the back of my throat. Cold chills have taken over my body.

She blinks.

Just once and slowly, but it's enough to send me flying back through the kitchen door. "She's moving. She's the only one moving. She blinked. She's moving." I lean on the counter for support.

The sound of the door swinging behind me makes my entire body go numb. I'm afraid to look. Panic sets in.

I turn my head a little, just enough to see a glimpse of long black hair and a white dress. That's enough to make me scream. I run for the back window. Screw this, I have no idea what they did but I'm not sticking around to see how it plays out. They're on their own.

My brother's hand on my arm stops me. "Christie—"

He's laughing. He's gone mad. He's—

"We got you so good," Emily says.

I freeze. "This was a joke?"

"Yup, and you fell for it," Matt says around the smile still plastered to his face.

My anger sends a rush of feeling back into my body. It's welcome after the panic. I usually hate being angry, but in this case it's so much better than the alternative. I breathe a sigh of relief. "You're both assholes, you know that right?" I shake my head. This is so like them, I should've seen it coming. I throw my hand at the door to the living room, indicating. "They're all just acting?"

"Yup. You should've seen your face," he manages between peals of laughter.

"Ok, fine, you got me. So who is this girl?" I point to the girl who is now right behind Emily. She is looking at me with a strange, blank expression. It's as if she didn't get the memo that the jig is up.

Emily looks behind her and then looks right back to me. Her eyes are questioning, her gaze blank. "What girl?" she asks.

She's serious, I can see it on her face as easily as I saw the panic earlier. Of course, that was fake so this probably is too. I force my eyes to roll. "Yeah, right. I'm not falling for that again. For real, who is it?" I take a step closer to the girl and hold out my hand. "I'm Christie, who are you?"

"Christie, what the hell?" Matt says. I turn my head to him, expecting the scared act again. Instead, Matt looks concerned. "There's no one there," he says. "Who are you talking to?"

"Stop," I say. The girl is still ignoring me. Still standing there as if she's alone. She tilts her head to the side, then further and further until her ear is touching her shoulder. Then she brings her hand up to her mouth in a "shhh" gesture before she opens her mouth and screams.

The sound is too high pitched to be normal. I reach up and cover my ears, trying to block the sound of the scream. It makes my entire body recoil and my ears vibrate.

When it stops, I pull my hands away and look at Emily and Matt. They're looking at me with concern. How are they not seeing this? "What is happening?" I yell.

The girl crosses the kitchen in two impossibly large steps. Before I can react, she flicks her wrist and all five burners of the stove come to life, engulfing the kitchen in flames. It spreads impossibly fast, roaring to life as if gasoline had been pooled on the floor.

The last thing I see before flames consume everything is the image of a girl in a long white dress floating out of the kitchen window, laughing as if she'd just pulled off the greatest Halloween prank ever.

Arresting

I believe we've already established my over-active imagination often leads to interesting scenes in my idea journal. This one is no different. Melded from things I have witnessed in my day job over the years with scenes from the news and things in my own imagination, this one is probably the most raw and real story in the collection. In a moment of trouble, can you trust the people sworn to protect and serve?

It's midday. The front of the store is flooded with natural light streaming in through the front wall of windows. The back of the store is flooded with that hum of fluorescent lighting. There are no customers, not right now. Two people have just left, they're actually still getting into their car out front.

The door opens and a new couple enters. They're about my age, which I'd like to call young but in reality, we're all old enough to have entirely too many adult expectations and responsibilities.

Both of the people entering the store are tall. He guides her through the door by putting his hand on her lower back, which is all kinds of adorable. I smile at them. "Good afternoon," I greet them. "Have you two been here before?"

He smiles. "No, ma'am, we have not. We just found this place."

I step out from behind the counter and the thick plexiglass, making sure my mask is covering my face. "Thank you for wearing masks today," I tell the couple. "What kind of books do you read? I'd be happy to show you where to find them." This is the store policy. When we have new customers, we show them to the right section. This is especially helpful because our store is huge and has everything.

"I read history," the woman answers. "He reads fiction."

"Let's take you to history first." I point out the general history section, the political history section, the section for Civil War, the section for English History, and the section for Black History. "I'll leave you to browse," I tell her, then turn to the man. "Follow me to fiction."

We round the corner and I hear the doorbell chime as we come near the fiction section. "Here's paperbacks for general fiction on your right and hardcovers of the same titles and authors on your left. They're loosely grouped by the author's last name," I tell the man. "If you need anything else, please don't hesitate to ask."

He is already looking at books so I step to the end of the aisle we're in. There's a new customer in the doorway. He's also about my age, but he's much larger. "Are you gonna make me wear a mask?" he booms.

"If you have one, I'd appreciate you wearing it," I answer truthfully. Then I add on the line I've been told to repeat. "The Center for Disease Control recommends one for all people in public settings."

"But are you going to make me?" he pushes. "Do you think a scrawny woman like you could force me to put this mask on?" He steps closer to me, bringing the man looking at fiction books into his view. I notice him taking in the other customer. He raises his voice. "Is there anyone in this whole store who thinks they could force me to wear a mask?"

The first man stands up fully. "I have no desire to force you to do anything. But I will echo her sentiment that I'd appreciate it if you did," he says. He makes no move to step closer to the confrontation.

"Did I ask you what you thought, nigger?"

My eyes slip closed at the word and I send up a little prayer for restraint from the first customer. I open my eyes and step between them. "Shawn, can I get a little help out front?" I yell. "Sir, I'm going to need to ask you to leave the store. You're being confrontational and that's not making anyone comfortable."

From behind the back counter come two other employees. Tracy, who is older and frailer than me, is shaking already. Shawn, the owner, is a 75-year-old white man. He's the only person I could think of calling. Staring at the two of them, I realize we are absolutely not equipped to deal with any situations that get out of hand. Fear dances up my spine.

Shawn wastes no time crossing to us. "Let's step outside," he says to the man. He pushes open the nearest door, which happens to be the one with no entry bell that is the least frequently used by customers.

"Are you kicking me out?" the man bellows.

"I just want to have a chat. See if we can figure out what went wrong here," Shawn answers. "Have a chat with me."

I don't hear the rest of their conversation because, thankfully, the man follows Shawn out of the store and shuts the glass door behind them.

I turn my attention to the man behind me. He is holding a book in his hand but hasn't moved a muscle since the last time I was looking at him. He is still standing straight up, facing toward the door. His jaw is clenched. "I'm very sorry. This is not the first impression we want to give you. Please accept the employee and family discount today. It's not going to make up for being disrespected, but it's literally the least I can do. I'm so sorry if this wasn't a pleasant shopping experience," I tell him.

"No problem." I notice his hands are balled into fists but he still doesn't move. "I appreciate that your store showed how you feel and that you are handling the problem." He turns his attention back to the books. The woman who came in with him steps into the aisle. "I'm fine," he tells her. "We're going to keep browsing and stay inside the store for a bit."

I straighten up and see Tracy has joined me in the aisle. We can still see Shawn and the man talking outside. "Does he look less agitated to you?" Tracy asks.

I take in the man's posture: arms slightly out from his body, leaning in toward Shawn. "No," I answer.

We're both watching as the man reaches under his vest and pulls out a gun. Tracy's sharp intake of breath matches my own. "Call 9-1-1," I tell her. He's not pointing it at Shawn. He's not pointing it at anyone. He's waving it around, gesticulating with it. Shawn seems entirely more relaxed than I would be, I'll give him that.

Beside me, Tracy is fumbling with the phone like it's a bomb she's trying to diffuse. "Do you want me to call?" I ask. She shakes her head, no she doesn't want me to call. Finally, I hear the ringing start through the loud handset.

She puts the device to her ear. "Yes, hi. I need a police officer at our bookstore. We have a man here who was upset about being asked to wear a mask and now he has a gun in the parking lot." She pauses. "I have no idea." She looks at me. "How can you tell if a gun is loaded?"

I shrug because the only way I can think of would be if the gun went off and I'd rather not think about that possibility right now. "We don't know," Tracy says into the phone. "Just send someone fast, please. There are other customers in the store."

She hangs up and we both stand there watching the parking lot as the minutes tick by. At one point another customer parks and exits her car. She moves to her passenger side to take out a walker, sets it up, and heads toward the door. Shawn steps back from the angry gun-wielding man to hold the door open for the woman. He intentionally chooses the one farthest away from the man so the chime goes off as she enters.

"Welcome in." My voice shakes as I greet her, trying to figure out the best way to proceed. I can't exactly ask her to leave past the dangerous situation she just came through. It's probably best to follow the lead of my new customers and keep things as normal as possible. "Have you been here before?"

"Many times," she answers. "I know my way around." She smiles at me and skirts right past me, headed for the romance section. It's the farthest section away from the door, which gives me an odd sense of comfort for her.

"Where are they?" Tracy whispers. It's been about three minutes, I would imagine. I don't know how long the police are going to take. In the parking lot, Shawn and the guy are just standing there. I don't know what they're waiting for. I just know I'd like the police to show up now.

The couple comes up behind me. "Excuse me, can we purchase these?" the woman asks.

I jump to attention. "Absolutely. I'm sorry again for the experience today," I tell them as we head to the counter. "I promise you it is not always this eventful." I scan in their books and punch in the employee discount. I give them their total and take the cash he offers.

"I think we should just have a seat here and start reading," he tells the woman. He gestures to a couple of chairs.

I look out the glass window and notice the car they brought to the store today is parked closer to the unused door, which means it's also closer to the gun-toting customer. I can't say I blame them for not wanting to walk by him. "Absolutely," I say. "That's what the chairs are for. Can I get you a bottle of water?"

Technically the bottles of water are for us, but I don't think Shawn would mind if I gave them away.

Both decline the water, sit in chairs, and open their books. He sits facing Shawn and the man outside while she has her back to the situation.

Finally, after what feels like hours, the police pull up. One car, two officers. They approach the two men in the parking lot and start having a discussion. The gun isn't put away. As far as I can tell, no one asks him to put it away. It's hanging loosely by his side now, pointing at the ground. I wonder if that is why they're not making a big deal of it. I wonder if they're afraid he'll point it at them like I'm afraid he'll point it at me, which is an absurd thought to have.

"Seems like they have it under control now," the man says. I jump at the sound of his voice. Then I smile to cover the fact that I had forgotten there were people here and that I was at work.

"It does seem that way," I say because they're all just standing in a little circle having a chat. It looks like four long-lost friends decided to get together at the bookstore today. No one looks agitated. No one looks jumpy.

"I think we're going to go," he says. They gather their belongings and stand.

I step out from behind the counter. "Thank you for coming in. I do hope you'll come and see us again. Things aren't usually this…" I fumble for a word. "… intense."

The man and woman leave through the door with the chime. I notice the police officers turn in their direction. One of them takes a step toward the couple. They stop and the man's hands instinctively go up in front of him. He shakes his head at whatever is being said and gestures toward his vehicle.

The police officer steps closer to him and pulls handcuffs off his belt. My feet move on their own, pulling me toward the door. There must be some kind of misunderstanding. Why would they handcuff this customer? But that's exactly what they do. The officer puts handcuffs on him and sits him on the curb. Shawn steps away from the armed man, gesturing at the black man and talking. I hope he's asking why. I hope he's clearing it all up.

"I'm ready now," a voice calls. I turn around to see the old woman with the walker standing at the register.

"Right, sorry." I go behind the register and check her out as fast as I can. My attention keeps getting diverted to the windows, but I'm too distracted to tell what's happening. It's like reading a comic book by only looking at the first picture on each page. Not enough information to figure out the plot.

"You're all set," I tell her. "Have a nice day and enjoy the books."

She turns and takes in the scene behind her. "Well, I can't wait for them to finish their business. I have a doctor's appointment." She fishes something out of her bag. "Would you be a dear and pull my car up to the door for me so I can go?"

I shouldn't. But, at the same time, I want her to be safe. I also really want to know what's going on out there. "I'll be right back," I tell her. "Wait here."

As soon as I open the door I realize things out here are not as calm as they seemed. For one, there's a lot of raised voices. For two, Shawn's face is a mask of anger and frustration. I couldn't tell that before because his back is to the store. His arms are outstretched toward the two situations that feel so separate. On his right, a black man is handcuffed and on the curb with an officer watching him, hand on the butt of his guy. On his left, a white man is pointing a gun at the ground while the officer beside him has his arms crossed over his chest. Everything about this feels backward.

"Ma'am, perhaps you should wait inside," the officer closest to me says. He's the one with his hand on the butt of his gun. That's where my eyes go. I force them back up to his face before I answer.

"There's an old lady with a walker inside. I'm pulling her car up so she can get back in. It'll just take a second." I look at Shawn. "I know it's not really policy—"

"We're operating outside of store policy right now," Shawn interrupts. "Get her car."

I rush off toward the purple vehicle she drove into the lot. I'm walking fast, but she didn't park far away. So I still hear Shawn say, "You know, I'd appreciate it if you'd let my other paying customer here get to his car like he asked to do."

"His baby mama is welcome to go get in the car but we're not done with him," a voice answers.

"We're already dealing with racism here," Shawn says. I'm shocked at how forceful and angry his voice sounds. "Let's not add sexism into the report."

I've reached the woman's car so I jump in, slam the door, fire up the engine, and pull to the front of the store. I leave the car running and the driver's door open. The old lady comes out and settles herself into the seat. I fold her walker and put it behind her seat. It's not where I saw her pull it from but it should work as long as she knows where it is. "Thank you," she says. "I hope your afternoon gets better than this." Then she drives off.

The scene in front of the store resumes as if they'd paused their act for her. There's a click from somewhere and something visibly changes in Shawn. His eyes snap to the man with the gun, and his entire body tenses. No one else reacts to the noise, whatever it is. The customer on the ground is still not moving or reacting. He is silently staring at the ground, his hands behind his back. His partner is standing beside him, her eyes focused on him. She is also not moving or reacting. They are the models for "stay quiet and do what you're told".

The man with the gun starts talking again. In the process, he is waving his hands. This includes the hand with the gun. I'm frozen in place, watching that thing wave around. I can't get my brain to focus on whatever he's saying. I've only seen a gun once before in my life and it certainly wasn't waving around. I notice the circles he's making seem almost centered on the black man on the curb.

Shawn must notice the same thing because he moves his body until it is between them.

"What are you doing?" The police officer closest to Shawn asks exactly what I was thinking. The officer closest to the gun-wielding man now has his hand on his hip as well.

"That man," Shawn points at the armed man, "just cocked his gun. I know you heard that. I had ten years in the military, I know that sound. Now he's waving it around. I want to make sure I'm standing between his armed and cocked gun and the customer who came into my store merely to buy a few books. If he's going to carelessly shoot someone I'd rather it be me than a paying customer."

I swallow. I try to get my feet to move but nothing happens.

The cop nearest the armed man takes a step closer. "Give me the gun, sir."

"Make me," the man barks.

Apparently, that is when he makes the first mistake of the day. It wasn't a mistake, in the eyes of this officer, to speak rudely to the employee and customer of the store. It wasn't a mistake to pull out a gun while talking to the owner of the same store. It wasn't a mistake to wave that gun, evidently cocked, around the owner, customer, and employees.

No, you just had to challenge the officer.

Because now the officer steps in and does exactly what the man asked him to do. He makes him give up the gun. In seconds the gun is in the hands of the police officer and the white man is in handcuffs. I feel my stress melting away, my shoulders dropping back down to where they belong Shawn's shoulders do the same. Then he turns to face the other situation. "Now, can we please let this man go? I'm not even sure what you're holding him here for. He is just a customer of the store. We can all give you statements."

"He was arguing with me," the officer with his

hand still on the butt of his gun, who has been watching the black man on the ground, says.

"He just asked to go to our car," the woman says.

The officer tenses. The man on the ground looks up. "Be quiet," he says toward his partner. "Please."

She nods.

Shawn takes a step toward the situation, slowly. I notice he puts his hands up. "If you can't see the racial tension here, take a step back and look at it like the media will look at it. An armed white man came into my store and caused problems. We refused service to him and asked him to leave at which point he became further agitated. Yet you arrived and spoke to him calmly and rationally. This man, who was merely shopping at my store peacefully and who didn't even speak unless spoken to, was immediately handcuffed and dropped on the curb. He already would have a pretty decent case for a lawyer to listen to and, if he's smart, he'll get your badge number before he leaves today. You can't fix what you've already done but you'd be smart to let him go before this gets any worse. He didn't do anything. He's a law-abiding citizen who was merely shopping at my establishment. Let him go."

"He's a witness," the cop pushes.

Shawn sighs. "I'm a witness and my employees

are witnesses. We all saw the original incident. We'll give you statements. The question is will we also be giving a statement about police brutality and racial discrimination?"

"He can go," the first cop says. "But leave your name and number if you want to leave a witness statement."

The second cop removes his handcuffs. The man stands up, rubbing his wrists. "Do you want to leave your name?" the cop asks.

"No, he doesn't," Shawn answers. "Which car is yours?" he asks. The man points to the green truck they arrived in. Shawn walks side by side with the couple, almost as if he's afraid of what may happen if he leaves them alone. At the car, Shawn follows the man to the driver's door while the woman goes to the passenger side. They exchange words none of us can hear. Then the truck drives off. It's out of the parking lot before Shawn comes back. "You'll need statements from all of us, I assume," he says to the officer.

"Eventually, yes. Another car should be here in about ten minutes. They'll get your statements entered into the record." He puts the once angry gun-wielding man into the back of the police car. "Have a nice day."

I realize I haven't moved during this entire exchange. I intended to, of course. I thought I would move that car and then get back into the safety of the store. Shawn must notice the same thing because he makes his way over to me. "We should get back inside," he says. "I'll have you and Tracy write out your statements before I close up the store for the day and send you both home. I think that's about as much excitement as we can handle."

"Where did you learn to say all those things?" I ask, not sure if that's the question I really want to ask but not able to think of anything else. He was so smooth out here. He kept his voice calm and stood up when he saw something wrong. It's a better reaction than what I did, which is freeze and panic.

Shawn sighs. "Too many stories show us what could go wrong. I had to try something to keep this one from getting worse." He pulls open the front door and holds it for me. "It could've been worse, you know."

"I know." There are so many examples I can call up that show me what worse can look like. No one was shot here today, that's important. Right there we're already better than so many of the stories. "Should we all wait for the police?" I ask. "Do you think a written statement will work?"

"I'll have you put a contact phone number on the bottom of the statement. I think we'd all feel better if we had a chance to write it out before we forget any details."

He walks behind the register and grabs a few notebooks and pens. He sets one of each down in front of me. "Just write what you remember."

I pick up the pen and notice my hands are shaking. They've probably been shaking since the loud man came in demanding I make him wear a mask. I hate confrontation. I don't deal well with it.

I realize I have to get this all written down before the emotions catch up with me and I fall apart. I do my best to record important facts and keep my opinion out of it. Then I write my name and phone number on the bottom of the paper.

Tracy is still writing. Shawn hasn't started, staring out at the now-empty parking lot. I hand him the paper. "Do you think this is good enough?" I ask.

He barely glances at it before he nods. "This is fine," he says. "Go home. I'll handle things here."

Part of me knows I should stay here in case anything else goes wrong. I should stay here, at least, until the second police car arrives to take our statements. But I can't stop thinking about all the things that could have gone wrong there and I need to get home and process all of this. I keep seeing that tall black customer putting his hands up and dropping down onto the curb as if he had done something wrong.

I grab my purse and head out to the employee lot. Then I pull out and drive by the front of the store on my way home. The sight of the spot makes me angry. What happened there was wrong, so wrong. I'm angry that no one wanted to listen until the white man told them to. I'm angry that they yelled at me and the other customers, but not really at the man with the gun. I'm angry that this happened at all.

I'm just angry.

Seb

I'm a Mom and I have two children. Someone once asked me how I would (or did) handle gender discussions with my kids. This short story was born from pieces of those conversations my children and I have had over the years. Are you the safe space someone trusts when it comes to big truths?

"Mom, this is Seb."

"Hi, Seb."

Dani's mom looks, and I'm not exaggerating, exactly like a TV mom would look. Her hair is pulled back in a twist and held with some kind of clip. Little wisps are freeing themselves and dancing around her face. She's dressed like she just came from work; black pants that hug her hips and legs, a white button-down shirt that covers everything that wouldn't be deemed office-appropriate, a long silver chain, a pair of glasses that magnify her eyes, and practical black flat shoes. I offer her my hand and she wraps it in both of hers, like a hug. "Nice to meet you," I mumble. It's almost painful to see women like this, women who were willing to make society work for them and not be crushed by it or run away.

She drops my hand. "Are you in sixth grade too, Seb?" she asks. Her eyes are fixed on my face. It's not like she's being rude, which I've seen my fair share of because even adults can be rude when they're faced with something they don't understand. Instead, it's like epic levels of eye contact. Like she's trying to show me that I have her undivided attention. Like I'm important.

Oof, powerful stuff this eye contact.

I swallow the emotions that are rushing at me. "Um, yeah. Dani's in my class."

Her eyes flit to Dani and then back to me. I think I see her smile drop just a fraction. "Dani?" she quips. "That's new."

"Mom," Dani whines. I mean, really whines. She draws out that O like it's the solo in a pop song. "I'm in sixth grade now."

"Right, you're right. It's your name. I'm sorry." She smiles at Dani and then goes back to me. "So is Seb short for something, too?"

"Um, yeah. But it's, like, a long story."

"I'd love to hear it. Do you want a glass of iced tea or something, girls?"

I wince at the assumption but before I can

even think about reacting, Dani is on top of it. "Mom, Seb doesn't identify as a girl. They're nonbinary. That means —"

Her mom stops her with a single hand, the most powerfully simple gesture I've ever seen. Dani literally swallows her word. "Seb, I'm so sorry I assumed anything about your gender. Thank you for correcting me. Would you like a glass of iced tea or something?"

"Iced tea would be great, thanks."

Dani smiles at me. "Are you sure?" she whispers. "My Mom can be totally nosey sometimes."

"Yeah, it's fine," I tell her. I don't tell her that her kind of nosey can be completely refreshing. I almost wish someone at home were nosey. The people at home don't care about me at all. It's easier for Dad if I just fade into the background. He doesn't understand me and he doesn't want to.

Dani and I sit at a big wooden table in front of the window. She sits with her back to the window but I sit where I can see the entire room and the backyard. The only thing I can't keep my eyes on is the cabinets behind me, which I can't imagine are going to do anything interesting. Dani's Mom brings three large glasses of tea to the table, sets one in front of each of us, and then sets a third to my right and sits down across from Dani.

"So, the long story for your name?" she

prompts, taking a big sip of the tea.

"Right." I also take a sip, trying to set myself up for what could be the end of this pretty picture we're painting. It's entirely possible her Mom is going to judge me right here. Understanding nonbinary and accepting it is one thing, although I'm not downplaying how amazing that is. Talking about choosing your own name and identity can get a little more real for some people. I'm fully expecting to see that uncomfortable shuffle of eyes and rapid swallowing. I take a deep breath. "So I was named Sabrina when I was born, which was my Mom's choice. I was always put in, like, pink clothes and bows and things, right? Which is, like, typical for little girls."

Her head tilts, questioningly. I wonder if this is the first sign she's becoming uncomfortable. I trudge on.

"But it didn't feel right to me. I'm not a girl. So, like, Sabrina didn't fit."

"That makes sense." She offers me a smile that, to her credit, doesn't look uncomfortable. "It's your name." That's the second time she's said that. I get the sense she really means it. It takes a second to get used to the change, like when her daughter suddenly decides she is going by Dani, but she accepts it. God, my Dad could learn so much from this lady.

"Anyway," I continue, "I thought maybe I was supposed to be a boy. The whole summer before third grade I wore clothes from my brother's room and told everyone to call me Sebastian. I guess I was, like, experimenting. I even think I started third grade going by Sebastian. My Dad was not happy with it, but he sort of let it happen."

"Seb's dad works a lot," Dani explains.

"That's an understatement," I mumble. Then I rush on with the rest of the story. "Anyway, boy wasn't right either. I don't really know how to explain this, honestly." I look down at the table and trace a line between two wooden planks with my finger. Try to figure out how else I can explain something that, to me, is only a feeling. Dani's mom's hand wraps around mine, there's no pressure. She's not stopping the tracing my finger was doing, just sort of doing it with me. Her hand is lightly there, but not pushing.

I look back at her face to find that same perfect smile, no discomfort. "You're explaining it perfectly," she says. "Nonbinary means exactly what you just said. I'm proud of you for taking the time to explain this to me."

My eyes well up with tears and I feel that burning in the back of my throat that means I might cry. I just feel so seen right now. I don't even think I realized how much I needed to feel seen until right this very second.

"So Seb isn't short for anything," she says. "It's something new. Born from the history of Sabrina and Sebastian, but better and stronger than them." She lets go of my hand and sits back in her chair. "Seb only needs three letters to contain all the awesome that either of those other histories had."

"Mom, quit," Dani says. I look her way and she rolls her eyes. "Mom writes advertising for a living so she's always thinking of ways to market and spin things. Even, apparently, your name. I'm sorry."

"It's cool," I tell her. I mean it. It is cool. She just figured out a way to perfectly describe my name. She gave words to something that, previously, only had feelings. This woman is magical.

"Alright, we're going upstairs now," Dani says. She pushes her chair back from the table and stands up. "Can I take this with me?" She points to the tea, still half full on the table.

"Don't spill it," Mom says. "Seb you can take yours, too."

"I won't spill," I tell her.

"The friends never do," she says. Then she winks. Really winks, like a movie star. Is there anything this perfect Mom can't do?

I follow Dani back across the floor toward the door we came in. "Seb," Mom calls from behind me. I stop, turn around, and find her standing exactly where we left her. "This is a weird question, I know, and stop me if you find it rude. But, do you need a hug?"

Again, I don't have words. I want a hug from this Mom so badly it's almost a physical pain. I have no idea what it feels like to be wrapped in a hug like that, the ones you always see on TV. But I don't know what Dani will think of me if I say I need one. Surely Dani has spent her whole life getting them. Won't that mean she thinks it's weird if I crave one?

I feel a little hand pushing on my lower back. "She gives the best Mom hugs," Dani whispers.

My feet move across the floor like they're being pulled by a magnet. At first, I'm hesitant. My arms are up away from me, but sort of hovering at her sides. Her arms wrap around my upper back, pulling me close. She smells like fabric softener and she's warm, and it gives the impression of hugging a batch of clothes fresh out of the dryer. She takes a deep breath and I feel her chest rise, then her arms squeeze a little.

Then it's over. She stands back and smiles at me. "Thank you. That story just made me want to hug you. You're an amazing kid, I hope people tell you that."

"You just did," I smile.

"Seb doesn't have a Mom at home," Dani reveals. "So they don't get embarrassing hugs and things on a regular basis."

Mom lays a hand on her chest. "Oh my gosh, I can embarrass you anytime you need," she offers. "I have enough embarrassment, grade harassment, stand-up-straight finger wags, and encouragement for more than my two kids." She leans closer to me and drops her voice like we're sharing a delicious snack of secret. "If you need to borrow a Mom, you've got me. Always and for anything. Okay?"

Again I feel that burn in my throat. "Yeah, okay," I tell her.

She straightens back up. "Alright, you kids go have fun. Don't do anything I wouldn't do and don't make a mess."

"C'mon, Seb," Dani calls. "This way to the video games."

"Love you," Mom calls as we make our way toward an impossibly thick-looking couch.

"Love you back," Dani calls.

I love the way she answers that like it's an automatic reaction built of years of routine. I can even imagine, someday, echoing that response right alongside Dani.

That's the House

Finally, we have the one that was inspired by a dream. I have dreams that take place "in my house". You likely know what I mean. In the dream, I'm as comfortable as I would be in my house. Yet, when I wake, I realize that it is not my house at all. Add that fact to my wild imagination and you have this story. Can you trust your dreams?

Monica stays in the car longer than she really should. She tells herself that if anyone asks she'll say she's listening to a good song on the radio. But, if she's being honest, it's that she doesn't want to deal with Grandma. That thought makes her feel small. Smaller than a crumb of cookie on the counter after Cookie Monster has had his way. This is her grandmother. The woman who gave life to her mother. If you can't count on family when you're at your lowest, who can you rely on to be there for you?

She gets out of the car, slams the door, and

clicks the lock function on her key fob. Then she moves into the building with purpose. The smile is adhered to her face before the woman in the lobby catches a glimpse of her. She pushes her sunglasses onto her head, shoving a few loose strands of her hair back with them.

"Hello again. Your grandmother will be so pleased to see you. She's looking at an old photo album as we speak," the nurse greets.

This particular nurse is always here on Thursday so Monica is not shocked at being recognized. She signs a sad excuse for her name to the visitor's log. "That's nice." Granny had been asking for a photo album pretty much since they checked her into the care center. The only one Monica could find was the one that, according to family legend, Gran made herself when Monica's mother was getting married. Monica cringes a little at the memory of the day she brought the album. Apparently, that album wasn't what Gran wanted. Despite asking for a photo album, for pictures, for memories, Granny practically threw the book across the room. It was only by luck that Monica had managed to hang onto the corner and keep the old book from falling apart. "She's looking at the album I brought? Is she finally coming around to it?"

"Nope, this one your brother brought by. I guess he found it in the attic? She's pretty happy about it." The nurse smiles as if this is good news.

Monica smiles back. She wonders if the nice nurse can tell the smile is fake. "I'll just go see what he's found, I guess. Thanks."

The entire walk down the cold hallway she's wondering why her brother didn't mention a photo album. Sure, they all knew she was looking for one, but why didn't he tell her he found one? Was it in Granny's attic? That would've been the first place she'd checked if she was the one living in the old house. She supposes she should be grateful he finally got around to looking. But she needed a little longer to be annoyed that it wasn't his priority when they first started the search. Sometimes, you just have to let anger simmer.

She rounds the corner and finds Granny in the old armchair. The sitting room here is loaded with natural light coming in from the lawn-facing windows. There are a handful of other people in chairs around the room, but her eyes go right to Granny. She's wearing a hand-knit shawl to fight off the chill of the air conditioning. On her lap is an open photo album. As Monica draws closer, she can see that most of the pictures are black and white. This is not an album she's seen before.

"Hi Gran," she says. She plants a kiss on the old woman's white hair and sits down on the ottoman beside her. "What's this you have here?" she asks. Her annoyance from earlier and her reluctance to come into this place have faded with the sight of the old woman. She takes her time looking over Gran's frame, happy to see that she looks well. She is dressed in comfortable clothes, pants that look like they'd be perfect for lounging about the house on a weekend, and a soft, light blue t-shirt.

Gran turns her eyes to her and smiles. There's no recognition there. Monica wills herself not to be offended. She points at the book. "Did Greg bring this to you?"

Those pictures are old. She doesn't recognize the people in them. Except—she points to one on the left-hand page. A young woman and a young man, his arms draped over her shoulder protectively. "Is that you and Grandpa?" Monica asks. The face is the same, although much younger.

"This is my Frank. Isn't he handsome?" Gran asks.

"He sure is. Where did Greg find this? Is this the book you've been asking for?"

"This is my book." Gran's frail fingers grip the top edge of the right-hand page. She slowly turns it, revealing more black-and-white pictures. On the center of the left page, the same couple stands with two small children at their feet.

"Is this Mom and Uncle Tom?" Monica asks, pointing again.

"That's my children." Gran turns back to face her, her eyebrows pulled together in confusion. "They're too young to have children."

Right. This is the reason it's painful to come in here week after week. Monica sighs and pats Gran's hand. She doesn't feel like trying to convince Granny that she's not a nurse today. Instead, she reaches up and turns to the next page, trying to draw Gran's attention back to the book.

Her breath catches in her throat. That house behind them. That's the house. "Where is this? Who's house is this?" She taps it with her finger in time with her quickening heartbeat.

"That's our house. It's in Virginia."

Gran hasn't lived in the house in Virginia in about fifty years. That's where she lived when they first got married. The twins were born there. The entire family moved to Arizona well before Monica was born. And Monica has never been there.

So why is this the house she's been dreaming of?

***

She's sitting at a kitchen table under a dim light. There's a cup of coffee in front of her, in a brown mug that looks handmade. Reaching out, she grabs the mug, wrapping her hands around it. She takes a sip of the coffee and sets it back down without really tasting it.

When her eyes flit back up, someone is standing in the room. She smiles. "Can I have a snack?" he asks. He's a boy, maybe ten. Part of her recognizes him, even if she can't place exactly who he is. She nods and he disappears with a pop. In his place, there's now a girl. Older, taller, but with the same basic features. "Can I borrow the car?" she asks, hand on her hip. Nod again and the girl disappears with the same pop.
This time a man is standing there. Old, frail, tired. His face is lined and he holds a hand out to her. "Still want to take a walk through the flowers with me?" he asks.

***

Monica wakes up in her dark bedroom. It takes a second for her brain to remember where she is. She's not at a kitchen table, she's in bed. She reaches for the little notebook beside her and squints at it. She should probably turn on a light to make this legible. But if she writes slowly maybe she won't have to.

Kitchen table—wooden and large.
Coffee cup—brown and maybe handmade?
Boy—Uncle Tom? Maybe around 10? Asks for a snack.
Girl—Mom? Maybe around 16? Asks to borrow the car.
Guy—Grandpa? Old? Asks to take a walk

She closes her eyes and tries to remember any other details from the dream.

Doorway behind the people connects kitchen to another room. Can see fireplace through doorway. Living room? Floors looked wooden all through. No carpet.

She runs her hands down her face. That's it. The dream is already fading. She tosses the notebook back on the table beside the bed and flops back onto her pillow. Monica has been dreaming of this house her entire life. In most of the dreams, it feels like a real place. She gets that weird dream sense of having been there before. In the dream, she always knows it's her house. Yet, it's not. Until this morning, she wasn't aware that it was a real house.

Now she's wondering what is happening. How is her brain feeding her dreams of her grandmother's old house? How much of her dream is reality?

She's going to have to spend more time with that photo album.

***

Monica's alarm on her watch wakes her at 6:30 the next morning. She turns it off and flips on her bedside lamp. Then she pulls the notebook to her and looks at what she wrote. She's pleased to find it legible, although unhelpful. Next, she grabs her cell phone from the charging plate and rubs her eyes as she brings the device to her face. A banner tells her she missed a call from Greg. Monica squints in confusion. Her brother never calls her.

She hesitates for only a heartbeat before hitting the banner to return the call. "Monica?" he answers. "Hey, thanks for calling me back."

"Of course. What's the problem?" She sits up fully in bed, willing herself to be awake enough for whatever crisis this call heralds.

"Not a big problem, sorry if I scared you. I just have a plumbing situation here and I need someone to come in. Do you remember the name of the guy who Gran always used? I think I should give him a chance first."

Monica resists the urge to scream into the phone and damage her brother's eardrum. Little things like this are exactly why she should be the one living in Gran's house. Her parents had decided it was important to the family to keep the house maintained instead of selling it. They don't want to sell the house out from under Gran while she's still alive, even if she can't make decisions right now. They also don't want it rented out to people they don't know or sitting empty when it can be bringing in money. Their solution was to offer it for a reasonable rent to the grandchildren. Greg had answered his damned phone first and taken the offer. Monica was nothing if not resentful. "Check her book."

"I did. There's nothing under P for plumber."

"It won't be under that. It'll be under his name."

Greg sighs. "I don't know his name."

"You'll have to go page-by-page and look for the word plumber next to it. That's the best suggestion I have."

"Fine. Thanks for nothing," Greg says.

"Hey, speaking of unhelpful," Monica transitions, "I heard you finally got around to looking for a photo album and found the right one in the most obvious of places."

"You're welcome."

"Why didn't you look weeks ago when I asked you to?" she pushes, suddenly eager to fight.

"Because I was busy, Monica, Jesus. Isn't the important thing that I found the fucking book and that it was the right one? She's happy right now. I don't want to talk about this." Greg's sigh is heavy and deep. "There's water in the fucking basement. I have to go."

Monica hears a rustle and then dead air. He's hung up on her. She throws the phone down on the bedspread. Water in the basement? That's probably not good. She wouldn't really know, of course, since she lives in the desert with the rest of her family. But Gran's house is up north, where basements can actually be added to houses. Basements that, she would assume, aren't supposed to fill with water.

Monica picks her phone back up and checks the weather for the last few days up near Gran's house. No rain. That just proves what a bad sign water in a basement is. She sighs. Not her problem. Part of living in that house means dealing with the things that happen in that house. This is officially a Greg problem. She shouldn't even know about it. He only called to tell her because he needed a phone number. What even made him think she'd have that number? She shakes her head, no she's not going down that rabbit hole. Greg can handle his problems himself.

She is going to get up, have breakfast, and go visit Gran. Sure, it's not her day. But suddenly she feels like a little visit with her Grandmother will cheer her up. If she happens to get another little glimpse into that photo album, even better.

***

"Well, this is a pleasant surprise." The receptionist greets Monica with a warm smile. "I didn't expect to see you today."

Monica tosses the excuses around in her head for a beat, deciding which one to offer. "We had so much fun looking at that photo album yesterday and walking down memory lane I thought it would be good to come back since I had time."

"That's nice, honey." The receptionist waits as Monica signs herself in and then hands her a visitor badge. "She's in her room this morning, but you can go on in."

Monica makes her way down the long hallway. She passes open doors, closed doors, and small inlets with water stations. It reminds her of her college dorm room. Of course, these residents aren't scurrying about to get to classes. They're mostly confined right here to this building. She can't think about that too much, it makes her sad.

She stops outside the door for room 638 and gently raps her knuckles against the frame. She isn't entirely sure what she's doing here today and figures the light knock will be her excuse to leave. If Gran doesn't hear it and welcome her in, she'll turn around and go. She'll tell herself Gran was getting a nap in and she didn't want to disturb her.

"Come in," a cheerful voice calls.

Monica plasters a smile on her face and pushes the door open. Gran, looking healthy and alert today, is standing at her sink. The water is off but her face is dripping a little as if she just washed it. She uses the towel in her left hand to wipe her face dry. "Oh, Monica honey. It's so nice of you to stop by for a visit."

For a moment, Monica can't breathe. She can't

remember the last time Gran recognized her never mind remembered her name. She shakes off her surprise, steps into the room, and pulls the door closed behind her. "Hi Gran." She steps across the small space, afraid at any moment the illusion will shatter and recognition will leave Gran's eyes.

When that doesn't happen, she holds her arms out and Gran steps into them. Monica almost tears up at the feeling of the old woman's arms tightening around her in a hug. "It's so good to see you," Monica says, her voice quavering. "How have you been?"

Gran pulls away and gestures to the armchair and the couch positioned in front of a television set that isn't on. "Let's sit and chat. Can I get you a drink?"

"I'll take a water," Monica says. She makes her way to the couch and sits, watching as Gran gets two glasses out of a cabinet and fills them both. The action is so typical it's almost painful. Monica can remember countless times in the past when she sat at the house Greg now lives in and watched Gran bustle about her kitchen making drinks and creating meals. It's comforting, this normal behavior.

Finally, Gran sits herself in the armchair and sets the drinks down on the table between them. "How is everything?" Gran asks. "How's the boyfriend, Steve, is it?

Oh, this is the Monica she remembers. The Monica of about four years ago. Monica who was engaged to Steven in finance. It's interesting, dealing with Granny's memory. Monica debates correcting her, telling her that Steven is no longer in the picture. He hasn't been in the picture for a long time. Instead, she keeps it simple. She can be this girl for her Gran. "He's good. Working hard. He's up for a promotion." At least he had been about four years ago. Monica wonders if he got that promotion or not. Wonders if he's doing well. "How are you doing, Gran? How's this place treating you?"

Gran waves her hand dismissively. "Fine. I'm always fine, you know me. I could stand a decent meal but I'm not complaining."

Monica smiles at the familiar sentence, almost always following a form of complaint. "I can bring you something next time I come. What sounds the best?"

Gran lays her head back on the chair and tilts her head as if the answer is written on the ceiling. "I would love a nice piece of warm cornbread with salted butter." She brings her face back to Monica and she is smiling. "Do you think that would be too much trouble?"

Monica has Gran's old recipe for cornbread at home. She even has the cast iron Mama used to make it in. This is an easy request. "No trouble at all, Gran.

I'll bring it by tomorrow." Beside Gran on the little square table, Monica spies the photo album. She gestures to it. "Hey, that's a nice-looking album. Can I take a peek?"

Gran grabs it, pulling it into her lap. "Oh, I love this one. I made this one right before we moved to Arizona. Your grandfather thought it was so silly of me to want a book just to showcase our life in Virginia, but it felt right to me. Have you ever been to our place there?"

"No, I haven't," Monica answers, scooting to the edge of her seat to look at the album with Gran. "You sold it, right?"

Gran purses her lips, thinking. "That sounds right. I'm sure we don't own it anymore. I don't remember the sale process. I'm sure your grandad handled all that. But you can probably still drive by it if you're ever out that way. It was a beautiful old house."

Monica can't imagine a scenario in which she would be in Virginia, to begin with. She certainly can't imagine a situation where she would be driving down a strange street to look at a house that she'd never been to before.

Gran points to a picture on the open page on her lap. "This is your Mom and her brother. They were the cutest babies."

Monica had seen this picture yesterday so she

ignores it. Instead, her eyes roam to the others on the page. She's looking for the kitchen from her dream or something else she might recognize. She reaches for the page edge when she doesn't find anything. "Are there any of you and Grandpa in here?" she asks, an excuse to get that page turned.

"Oh, I'm sure there are." Gran lets Monica turn the page and flattens it down to the one before it in the book.

Again, Monica's eyes quickly roam the page. She finds a picture of Gran and Gramps in front of the house, smiling. The hair on her arms stands up. She points a shaking finger at the picture. "Is that Gramps?" she asks, already knowing the answer.

She can hear the smile in Gran's answer. "Yes, that's him. Such a cute man."

"That's a heavy-duty old mug he's holding. It almost looks like someone hand-made it for him."

"You have such a good eye, sweet girl. I went through a ceramic phase. I took a class in the community center to give myself something to do when your mom and Uncle were born. I made two mugs, a matching set. We both used them every day. You know, I'm not sure where they got off to. I bet they didn't make the trip from Virginia."

Monica, who has washed most of the dishes in Gran's house by hand because they never had a dishwasher, is relatively certain that is true. So that makes it even stranger that Monica is positive that is the mug from her dream.

No doubt about it, she's dreaming of Gran's house and Gran's mug.

But why?

***

She steps out of the car and shuts the door, looking up at the house. Everything inside is dark and quiet. She makes her way up the walkway and unlocks the door. The lights are all off and the curtains are drawn. She sets her things down and opens the two sets of curtains in the living room, letting light in.
She turns on the television and flips to the news station. She likes to have the news on in the background while she's cooking dinner. She makes her way across the house, leaving her shoes by the door as she walks by. In the kitchen, she opens the refrigerator and starts to take out ingredients, setting them on the island behind her.

***

Monica startles awake, her arm flopping off the bed toward the floor. She takes a few deep breaths to calm her racing heart. The feeling of falling out of bed is always the worst. She rolls over, trying to get comfortable again. Was she just dreaming about her grandmother's house again? She tries to recall the dream before it can fade. It felt like her house, the way it always does in a dream. She was comfortable and moving around. She turned on the news, but it was an older television, one where she walked up and pressed the button instead of hunting for three remotes. She flips to her back and stares at the ceiling. It wasn't her house or her television. It was Gran's, she's pretty sure. So, again, she was dreaming about being in Gran's house for some reason. But it felt more recent, somehow. She closes her eyes and tries to remember the details that made her think it was recent. She got out of the car, but she didn't look back at it. She opened the front door with a key, but she didn't notice any key chains.

The house was empty and dark, she recalls. Empty because Gran was coming home to an empty house? Because Grandpa was already gone? Maybe that's what she's thinking of.

But, wait, is that what she thinks is happening? Is she dreaming of things that Gran would remember? Things that Gran would have memories of?

That's ridiculous.

More than likely, it's Monica trying to assign memories to things she saw in that photo album. Yes, that's it.

But she saw the picture of the mug after she dreamed about the mug.

No, that can't be right. She must have seen the

mug the first time she looked at the photo album, it just didn't register in her mind. Brains are smarter and faster than people. Brains are recording and observing millions of things every minute whether people notice or not. Her brain is always cataloging things and making connections. She saw that photo of the mug and then her brain filled in where it might have been used. The same thing is probably true about the television, the car, and the refrigerator. Next time she's with Gran she'll probably see pictures of those things. The truth is, those things have been there all along.

Monica rolls over and pulls the blanket tighter, content that she's found an answer that makes logical sense.

A few hours later, the watch on her wrist begins to chirp and vibrate. When Monica doesn't wake up and turn it off, both the volume and the intensity increase. Eventually, it pulls her from sleep and she hits the button to tell it that she's awake. Then she stretches in bed, feeling that satisfying pop in her neck and shoulders. She reaches for her phone and remembers she had another weird dream.

Instead of the phone, she grabs the journal where she records her dreams that she wants to remember. Nothing is written there. Strange, she thinks. She was pretty sure she dreamed of Gran's house last night. Something about a car and the news being on. She can't remember anything else. Setting the journal down with a shrug, she switches to her cell phone.

She scrolls through her messages and emails, unwilling to get out of bed yet. It's been her habit for a few years to get up earlier than she needs to so that she can spend a little bit of time under her covers in comfort before it's time to get going. It's one of her favorite parts of the day, even if she still hates getting out of bed.

Her phone starts ringing in her hand and the screen lights up with the number of her grandmother's care facility. "Shit," she mumbles. She assumes this is not good news this early in the morning. She swipes to answer. "Hello."

"Hi, this is Nancy from your grandmother's place. I just wanted to call because I wasn't sure if you were planning to come up today and I didn't want you to be shocked when you came in. Today has been a bit of a struggle." She says all of this is a kind of rush, probably eager to make sure Monica doesn't think something drastic is wrong.

"Oh," Monica says. "What's going on? Is everything ok? Is Gran feeling ok?"

"Yes, oh gosh I'm sorry to worry you. Her health is good. I just didn't want you to come into a shocking situation. She's not remembering much of anything today. It's been a struggle to get her to recognize where and who she is."

For a beat, Monica considers skipping the visit today altogether. If it's hard for this stranger to deal with it, imagine how hard it would be for Monica. But that's not fair to this nurse or Gran. "Thank you," she says. "I appreciate the heads up. I think I'll get dressed and see about coming in early. Maybe seeing a friendly face will help. Plus, I promised her some cornbread."

"Yeah, that's fine. I hope it's alright that I called."

"Perfectly fine, Nancy. Seriously. Keep my number with you and call whenever you need to. I appreciate you looking out for her."

"Great. See you soon."

Monica hangs up the phone, texts her boss that she's going to come in a little late but that she'll stay late to make up for it, and drags herself to the closet. She can't explain why she feels the need to be with Gran so much this week. It must be the dreams. Dreaming of that house is making her feel inexplicably closer to her grandmother. It's nice, she supposes. Who knows how many more days they'll have to spend together? Monica can always work too many hours when Gran is gone. For now, she wants to spend time together.

***

After signing into the facility, Monica makes her way to her grandmother's room. The door is open and there's a man in a white coat inside. Monica knocks gently on the open door. "Can I come in?" she asks. "Is this a good time?"

"Of course, come on in," the doctor says. Monica doesn't recognize him. He's tall and has a confident air about him. "We were just having a little chat about Alicia's medical history and reminding her why she is here in our facility. Would you like to join us and introduce yourself?"

Monica hates that this is necessary but she settles herself in the empty armchair facing Gran. "I'm Monica. I'm your daughter Tanya's oldest child."

There's no recognition there in Gran's eyes at the mention of her children. This is new. Usually, something triggers a spark in her eyes. Even if she can't remember her grandchildren, doesn't she remember her children? Monica's eyes catch on the photo album sitting on the table beside Gran's chair. She gestures to it. "Can I show you?" she asks.

When Gran doesn't protest, Monica takes the book and flips open the heavy cover. "I know it can be frustrating to not remember," she says. "But maybe these will help." Monica points to the picture that is becoming so familiar to her. "This is you and your husband, do you remember him?"

"That's my house in Virginia," Gran says. "It's a beautiful old place. I love being there but when I'm alone it's too quiet."

"You turn on the news for background noise," Monica says without thinking.

"That's right. I do." There's the spark of recognition. The news is the connection. This memory is a shared one for now.

"Why would you be in the house alone?" Monica asks. "Where's Grandpa?"

"Oh, I don't know. Work or something, I'm sure. It's fine. I don't mind being alone most of the time. It's just that the house makes noises because it's still so new to us. I'm sure after a few years of living there, I'll get used to all the noises." She sits forward in her chair, perching herself on the edge. "Do you think they'll let me go home soon and check on the house?"

Oh, this is the version of her grandmother she gets today. The woman who was a wife before she was a mother. The woman who was a new homeowner. She lived in Virginia and probably had a whole life of her own that Monica knows nothing about. Monica swallows. "Well, I'm not sure. But I can go check on it for you," she says. Her voice catches a little on the lie. "I'd be happy to do that."

"Oh, would you?"

"Absolutely." Monica reaches for her purse. "Actually, I brought you something because the last time I was here you asked me to. Would you like a piece of cornbread?" She pulls a storage bag out of her purse and holds it up for Gran to see.

"Cornbread is one of my favorite foods," Gran says. "But I have a special recipe so I'm a little picky."

"Why don't you try mine and see how it compares," Monica offers. "My recipe is from my grandmother." She doesn't remind her, again, that she is the aforementioned relative. It's too painful to do that. Instead, she unzips the bag and holds it out.

Gran leans in toward the bag and takes a big sniff, testing the smell. "It certainly smells good," she says. Then she reaches her hand in and pulls out a square. She pushes it gently between her fingers. "Good texture." She takes a small bite, chews, and swallows. "Heavens, that is good. If I didn't know better I'd say it was my own recipe." She turns to the doctor, still standing by the kitchenette counter. "Would you like a piece of cornbread?"

He waves her off. "I'm all set, thanks. I had a big lunch. I need to be going. Monica, can I borrow you for just a quick second?"

Monica stands up and follows the doctor out into the hallway. "I'm sorry about this," he says. "It can be difficult when the memories are not coming. Thank you for being patient with her. I do want to caution you about making promises. Likely she won't remember them, but I'm not sure you plan to travel to Virginia and I'd hate to irritate her if she does remember it."

"I know, I felt bad about saying that. I just didn't know how else to ease her mind. I think they sold that house. Even if I wanted to visit it, I couldn't."

"Don't let it bother you. You're doing well in there. Call the front desk if you need anything."

"Thanks, doctor." Monica shakes his hand and watches him walk down the hallway before she returns to the room. She doesn't want to make Gran worse, but she can't imagine not promising something so simple if it will ease Gran's mind.

Back in the room, Gran is eating what appears to be a second piece of cornbread. "Do you need a glass of water to wash that down?" she asks.

"That would be great, Monica dear."

The voice sounds different, somehow. It's still Gran's voice but something about it sounds more sure and solid. Monica stares at her, blinking. "Gran?" she prompts.

"Yes, dear?"

"Are you ..." she trails off, trying to figure out how to phrase this. You can't exactly ask if you're remembering things. That's not how this works. Monica swallows. "Are you enjoying the cornbread?

Is it the right recipe?"

"Sure tastes like mine," she says. "I'd say you did it just right. Did you use my old cast iron or did you finally get one of your own?"

Monica wants to run across the room and hug her. The only version of her grandmother who would know about the cast iron and that Monica didn't own one is her grandmother. The one she remembers. A recent iteration. She forces herself to get a glass out of the cabinet and fill it with water before making her way across the little room. She sets the glass down. "I used Mama's old one," she says. "I still need to get one. Maybe I'll treat myself for Christmas."

Gran smiles. "You should. Proper cast iron is an investment that is worth the upfront cost, love." She takes a big drink of water and sets the glass back down. Then, she gestures at the photo album. "Where did this old thing come from?"

Monica fingers the page. "Oh, Greg found it in your attic. He thought you'd like to see it. Take a little walk down memory lane."

"That's the old house."

"In Virginia," Monica prompts.

"I've said that a time or two, have I?" Gran laughs. "Hard to remember what I've said and what I haven't said with this foggy brain of mine."

"It's fine," Monica says. Because what else are you going to say? Can't very well explain to your grandmother that it hurts every time you have to start over with a conversation. "I like hearing about it." She reaches out and gets herself another slice of the cornbread, putting it on a napkin. "When did you move from Virginia?" she asks.

Gran frowns, perhaps trying to remember. "Just after the twins were born. Grandpa and I decided it was best to be closer to family and his brother already lived out here in Arizona. So he packed up our stuff and drove it across the country. I came along with the children once he was here and settled."

"Then you sold the house?"

"You know, I can't remember. I'm sure we did but I don't remember handling any of that. Your grandpa, he did it all." She takes another bite of her cornbread. "That's how things were back then, you know. We let them handle all the things related to paperwork. We handled everything else."

Monica takes a bite of her cornbread to cover her eye roll at the traditional marriage roles conversation. "I actually had a dream that I was in your house in Virginia," Monica says. "More than one dream, believe it or not. I almost feel like I know the house now after all these dreams."

"It was a beautiful house." Gran sighs. "I could've stayed there forever if we didn't need help with the twins."

For some reason, that sparks the dream from last night to flit across Monica's brain. In the dream she'd been alone in that house, she thinks. Something had given her that impression anyway. The dark windows when she came home, maybe. She'd turned on the news for background. Maybe this had been during a time when Grandpa was driving across the country, intent on moving to Arizona. But then why would the babies have not been home? "Gran, was there ever a time when you would've been coming home to that house alone?"

"Alone?" Gran scrunches her eyes up in confusion. "Probably. Why do you ask?"

"I don't know." Monica takes another bite of cornbread to buy herself a little time to think of how to phrase this. "One of those weird dreams was coming home to a dark house. No one was home, no lights were on. I came in and turned on the news for a little background noise before heading to the kitchen."

"I used to do that," Gran exclaims, her eyes light up with the memory. "I hated the sound of an empty house. My Frank used to tell me I was wasting the electricity," she sort of laughs. "But he couldn't tell me that when he wasn't home."

"So there were times when you might have done something like that?"

"Well of course. You aren't glued to the hip of

your spouse after you get married, Monica." Gran smiles at her to soften the blow of the implication that Monica is being naive. "Sometimes Frank would work late and I would come home to an empty house. There were even a few times when he traveled out to meet his brother and scope out Arizona before we moved. I suppose after the twins were born I would have been coming home with them, but I spent plenty of time alone in that house."

There's a soft knock at the door. "Come in," Gran calls. The door opens and a nurse Monica recognizes pokes her head in.

"Sorry to interrupt," she says, "but Alicia's got physical therapy so I need to escort Monica out."

"Oh, is it that time already?" Gran asks.

Monica is startled to find she doesn't want to go. Her grandmother is engaged in this conversation right now and active in the memories. She doesn't want to leave while that is happening. Of course, she isn't going to argue with the facility and she knows this isn't going to last. She stands. "I'll come back tomorrow," she promises. "I love you."

"I love you too, honey. Take care of yourself."

They hug and Gran kisses her cheek before Monica is led out the door by the kind nurse. "She seemed to be doing well there just now," the nurse notes.

Monica nods. "It was coming back to her a

little. This was a good moment."

"Good." The nurse lays her hand on Monica's arm. "Have a good rest of the day. You know the way out, I'm sure."

Monica nods and takes off in the direction of the lobby. Her brain is whirring. It almost sounded like the dream she had was a memory of Gran's, but that doesn't make sense. How would Monica have known enough about Gran's life in Virginia to not only be dreaming about the house but actually be dreaming of Gran's past?

She shakes her head, hoping it will send the strange thoughts scattering. She should focus on her waking life, instead of getting lost in a dream world. She has to go into the office, get some paperwork done, and call her brother to see if he figured out the plumber's contact information even though she shouldn't be helping him and it's definitely his problem. She doesn't have time to analyze her strange dreams.

By the time she's in the car, she's pushed all thoughts of the dreams out of her head.

***

The coffee in the mug is hot and delicious. She sets the mug down and sighs, content. The corded phone on the

wall starts ringing. She stands, going to the wall, and picks up the receiver. "Hello," she greets.
"Hi, this is Charlie at work. Can you possibly pick up an extra shift for me today? I have to leave early and I was supposed to close. There's been a minor issue with my kid at school. He's fine but he has to be picked up."
She checks the clock above her stove. "I can be there in fifteen minutes," she says.
"You're the absolute best. Thank you."
"No problem." She hangs up the phone and opens a drawer by her hip, pulling out a pad of paper and a pen. She writes out a quick note in slanted handwriting. "Gone back to work to pick up a shift for Charlie. Don't wait up." She signs it only with a heart and leaves it by the coffee pot.
Then she makes her way back to the table, picks up her mug, and drains it in one gulp.

***

Monica's eyes flutter open without the usual shock at the dream ending. She rolls over and reaches for her journal. She scratches out a few notes in the dark, squinting at the paper.

Worked with Charlie. Picked up shifts sometimes. Left notes for Grandpa signed only with a heart. Handwriting looked different from mine, more slanted and flowing.

Confident she recorded everything she could remember, she lays her head back down and returns to dreamland.

When the alarm clock on her wrist pulls her out of sleep a few hours later, she stretches and checks the note. Her phone rings and she picks it up, tilting the screen in her direction. She groans before thumbing the button to answer it. "Yes, dear brother," she says with an annoyed tone to her voice.

"Hey, I found a plumber to come look at this but they're quoting me like $800 for the repair. Do you think I could, maybe, borrow a little money? I know it's a lot to ask."

Monica runs her hand down her face and closes her eyes wishing she could just rewind to five minutes ago when she was asleep. Why does Greg always manage to call just as she's waking up? With her eyes closed, she can almost feel the tug of sleep pulling her back under. "Just call Leonard, he'll give you a good price," she mumbles.

"Who the hell is Leonard?" Greg asks.

Monica's eyes fly open. "What?"

"What?" Greg echoes.

"Did I say something about a Leonard?" She blinks rapidly trying to clear the sleep from her eyes. She definitely said that. But where did that information come from? Who is Leonard? She can't remember knowing that name. She can't remember the seconds that led up to her coming up with that name.

"You sure as hell did. Is this some kind of

joke? When I called you a few days ago to ask for Gran's plumber's name you didn't know it. Now all of a sudden you come up with a name?"

"Do you think that's the plumber's name?" she asks, just as confused as her brother is.

"I don't know. I'm walking to the book now." She can hear her brother flipping pages in something, likely Gran's address book. "I started at the beginning of this stupid book and looked through every entry but I didn't get to the Ls," he mumbles. The page flipping stops. "Oh my God, you're such a bitch."

"What? Why? What did you find?" Monica sits up.

"Leonard Franklin, plumber." He lets out an angry roar. "Why didn't you just tell me that the first time? It would've saved me time. Never mind, thanks for nothing. I'll call Leonard. Maybe he can do it cheaper."

"I'm sorry. I swear I don't know where that came from," Monica says, but the other end of the conversation feels quieter, suddenly. She pulls the phone away from her ear and sees her home screen. He hung up on her.

She drops the phone on the bedspread and sits back against the headboard. How in the world did she pull that name out of her brain? She's pretty sure she's never heard Gran mention the name of her plumber before. Sure, she may have heard it in passing over the years. It's a common enough name. But it's not a name she ever would have associated with Gran's plumber. Plus, if it's something her brain was going to recall wouldn't it have been more helpful to recall it when Greg called asking for that information?

"This is getting really weird," she mumbles out loud. First, she was dreaming about the house. Then, she started noticing the dreams seemed to be actual memories of Gran's. Now, when she closes her eyes and unfocuses on the conversation she can remember details only Gran would know. What is going on?

She needs a test. Something she is certain she doesn't know. The notebook beside her is still open to the page from last night. Gran worked with a Charlie but what company did they work for? This isn't something Monica would know. For as long as she's known Gran, she's been retired. She's pretty sure Gran stopped working when they moved out here, preferring instead to be a stay-at-home mother and raise her children. Monica couldn't name a single profession Gran had ever been in, let alone any of the companies she worked for.

Monica closes her eyes, leans back on the pillow, and breathes deeply. She tries to stop thinking about anything and just focuses on her breathing. She's letting herself get worked up about something stupid. She just remembered a name Gran had told her before and got lucky that it was the right name. It'll be fine. This is normal. She's fine.

She's being pulled back toward sleep again, aware that there will be no alarm clock to bring her back around in time for work.

Tiger Tales Bookshop.

Monica's eyes fly open. With a shaking hand, she reaches for the pen and notebook. She writes down the name. She absolutely has to go into the office today and get things done but she also knows she has to go visit Gran again today.

She needs to fact-check this information.

She sort of hopes it's wrong.

***

Monica sets the small notebook on the table between the armchair she's chosen and the one Gran is occupying in the lobby of the care center. "Can I show you something?" she asks. She's been here for about fifteen minutes already with the notebook carefully tucked in her purse. She was hoping to have another visit where Gran was coherent and remembered Monica in some form. That's not happening. Instead, Monica has played the "visitor" or even "employee" role today. Still, she can't leave without at least asking about the things she's been dreaming about.

"Sure, dear," Gran answers. Her smile is hesitant as if she's expecting Monica to ask for something completely out of pocket and have to turn her down.

"I have a few things written in here," she gestures to the notebook, "I wanted to see if they mean anything to you. Can I read them out?"

"What kinds of things?" Her grandmother tips her head to the side, cautious.

Monica flips open a page, leaving the book between them in case Gran wants to see what really written. "House has a large tree in the backyard. A rope hangs from it," Monica reads.

"You want to know if that means anything to me?" Gran asks. "I have a tree in my backyard but, dear, a lot of people do."

"Sure." Monica turns a few pages to a later dream. "Kitchen table is wooden and large. Coffee cup is brown and handmade." She looks up at Gran's face in time to catch that glimmer of recognition again, as she did the last time the mug was mentioned.

"I have a mug like that," she says. "I did make it myself, actually. I took a ceramics class when my babies were small."

"That's interesting," Monica says.

"Where did this notebook come from?" Gran looks skeptical now, possibly even concerned.

Monica doesn't want her to get upset or refuse to speak with her. She thinks fast. "I'm not sure who it belongs to. We found it and we're trying to figure out who may own it."

"Well it doesn't look familiar but those things are things that I remember. It must be someone of a similar generation to me. Maybe a neighbor."

"Maybe," Monica says. "This should help clear that up." She flips to the most recent page with trembling fingers, almost afraid to ask about this one. "Does the name Charlie mean anything to you? Or, perhaps, Tiger Tales Bookshop?"

Her grandmother's entire face lights up in a smile and she nods happily. "Oh, that makes complete sense," she says.

"It does?"

"Yes, the book will belong to Charlie. She's my good friend and coworker. I'm sure she probably has a brown mug like that as well, she is the one who recommended the ceramics class and she's always drinking coffee." She chuckles. "I hope that helps. You can find Tiger Tales and return that to her. If I'm not there, she must be working. We almost always cover alternate shifts for each other. I should find out when I'm scheduled next, actually." Gran starts turning her head left and right as if looking for someone whom she can ask.

"You took some vacation days," Monica says, laying her hand on Gran's knee. "Charlie must be covering for you."

"Oh, well, be a dear and thank her when you return her notebook." Gran sits back, relaxing. "I'm so glad we figured that out."

Monica, however, is not so glad. The problem is becoming clearer, even if she can't figure out how to solve it.

When she dreams, even daydreams, she is inside of Gran's lost memories.

***

Monica pulls into her mother's driveway and turns off the car. She'd called her Mom at work today, more than hinting that she had something important to tell her. She'd scored herself a dinner invitation easily. Now, sitting in the solace of the car and thinking about what she wants to bring up, Monica isn't sure why she thought she could do this. Her mother isn't the "dreams are important" type. She's going to think this is a load of hogwash. Plus, knowing Monica thinks it's true is likely only going to make her angry. This is a mistake.

Still, Monica can't very well turn the car

around and leave. Mom was expecting her and she probably saw her pull into the driveway. She unbuckles and gets out of the car, plastering on a fake smile. She'll make up some garbage to tell Mom about. She'll avoid the actual issue. Mom can't handle it. It's as simple as that.

An hour or so later the center of the table holds three-quarters of what was once a full pan of lasagna and only about a quarter of what was once a full bottle of wine when Monica accidentally lets the plumber conversation slip. She lets out a loud exhale and rolls her eyes at herself.

"What did he need a plumber for?" Mom asks. "Is something wrong with Mom's house?"

"No, no. I'm sure it's fine. There was water in the basement or something. But he's handling it. The plumber is handling it."

"But Mom has a plumber she likes. Did he call the right guy? I'm sure I have his number somewhere here. He should've called me."

"Right, can you tell him that?" Monica asks. "I don't know why he insists on calling me and I sure as heck don't know why he keeps calling me in the morning. I'm not exactly at my best in the morning, you know? He could call at night or something. I don't know." During her rambling answer, she notices her Mom has picked up her phone and has been texting. She briefly wonders who she's talking to, but decides not to ask. Instead, she reaches for the bottle of wine and empties the last of it into her glass.

"How did you know the name of the plumber?" Mom asks, turning her phone toward Monica. The screen shows a text stream between Greg and Mom.

"Shit," she mumbles.

"What are you not saying?" Mom sets the phone down. "Talk to me."

"So, I've been having these dreams," Monica starts. She takes a big sip of her wine to give herself time to think of what comes next. "Of Grandma's house in Virginia and some other things."

"That's strange. You've never—"

"Been there," Monica finishes. "Right. That's what I thought when I saw the photo album Greg found. Then, it got weirder."

"What is that supposed to mean?"

Monica takes a deep breath and lets it out through dramatically pursed lips. "I'm just going to jump to the conclusion and you can judge me all you want." Mom nods. "I think I'm dreaming of things that Gran lived. I think I'm dreaming of her lost memories and I don't have to be fully asleep for it to happen, either."

Mom stares at her. Monica counts four blinks before she takes another swig of her wine. Once she sets her glass down, she counts another six blinks. "You gonna say something?" she finally prompts.

"How?" Mom shakes her head. "I mean, what?" She shakes it again. Then she reaches up and rubs her hands down her face. The gesture makes her look incredibly tired. "Tell me why you think these are memories and not dreams," she finally settles on.

"Right, so I obviously can't be sure. But I have pulled information out of them that I couldn't possibly know otherwise that Gran has confirmed is true during some of her lucid times. Things like watching the news in an empty house—"

"Everyone does that," Mom interrupts.

"Or using a hand-made brown mug she made in ceramics, or working with a woman named Charlie at a place called Tiger Tales Bookshop, or the name of her plumber."

"Those are harder to explain," Mom concedes. "I don't think I understand. Why would you be dreaming these things?"

Monica laughs. "I have no idea. I was hoping you'd have some insight."

Mom reaches across the table and snags Monica's wine glass, taking a big swig. "This is weird."

"Completely." Monica waits a few beats. "Do you believe me?" she asks, her voice quieter than it was before.

"I believe that you honestly think something strange is happening. I believe you're dreaming. I'm not sure if I believe they're memories. But it is strange." She reaches across the table again, this time covering Monica's hand with her own. "What do you want me to say?"

Monica shrugs. "I don't know. I guess I just wanted someone else to know it was happening. I feel better already." It's not entirely a lie, Monica realizes. She does feel better knowing that someone else in the world knows she's having these dreams. But it doesn't help her get anywhere near figuring out why it's happening. That is something she'll need an expert for.

***

Good Afternoon,
I found your information after a little Google search. It
appears that you are something of an expert in the field of
dream interpretation. I live in the valley but I will be up in
Sedona this weekend and I'd love a chance to meet with
you. Would something like that be possible?
Monica Alders

***

Monica checks the address again before opening the door to the new age store in Sedona the following Saturday. A bell over the door announces her entrance and someone deep within the store calls out a greeting. Monica makes her way to a counter where she finds a young girl working behind the register organizing cards of some kind. "Hi, I had a meeting scheduled with Somer," Monica says.

"She's in the back." The girl gestures behind a beaded curtain to her right.

"Am I allowed to just go back there?" Monica asks. "I've never been here before."

"Yup, help yourself."

Feeling incredibly awkward, Monica pushes through the curtain and into a little hallway that breaks off into two rooms, one on either side. "Hello?" she calls. "I'm looking for Somer. I have an appointment."

"Right through the door on your right," a voice calls.

Monica takes the doorway on the right, as instructed. A dark-haired young woman sits on a wheeling chair in front of a relatively normal-looking desk. Monica isn't sure what she expected, but it's not this. First, the girl is younger than she would've guessed. How do you get to be an expert on dreams if you are barely old enough to be an expert on anything? Then there's the desk. Everything about it looks corporate. There are two paper sorting baskets, exactly the kind Monica has on her own desk, a pencil holder, a laptop computer, and a phone.

Nothing looks out of place.

The girl stands and offers her hand across the desk. "You must be Monica."

"I am, are you Somer?" Monica shakes her hand.

"That's me. Why don't you have a seat and tell me what's going on?" Somer gestures to the empty chair across from the one she is hovering over. Once Monica sits, she copies the gesture.

Monica does her best to keep the explanation short. She mentions the same facts she used to try to convince her mother, making sure to tell Somer she hadn't known about these things before the dream. Then, because Somer's easy smile makes her feel less like she's being judged, Monica tells her the full story of pulling the plumber's name out of her brain while she was half-asleep.

Somer nods as if this is all making perfect sense. "Your grandmother has Alzheimer's, you said?"

"Correct."

"How advanced is her disease?"

"She's in a care facility because her memory isn't reliable." It's the easiest explanation.

"So it's fair to say these memories you're dreaming of are not memories your grandmother has ready access to right now?" Somer pushes.

Of course, Monica had the same thought. But hearing it out loud is interesting. She didn't say it first. If two people come to the same conclusion without influencing each other, does that make the conclusion stronger? Monica would like to think so. "I would say that's fair."

Somer folds her hands and sets them on the desk. "Dreams are our brain's way of processing things we are unable or unwilling to process when we are awake," Somer begins. "Sometimes they can be emotions, like fear. Sometimes they can be situations we didn't fully reflect on during the day. Sometimes they can be seemingly random or hard to decipher. I think, in this case, we're quite lucky. The meaning is clear. Someone has to be responsible for those memories and your brain has decided you'll be handling that."

"So you don't think they're real? You think my brain made them up?"

Somer takes a deep breath as if pulling the answer from the oxygen in the room. Then she smiles. "I think the science behind it would tell us that, on some level, you do know these things. Someone once told you a story or you heard about it, maybe even unconsciously. Now, because you're worried about the memories being lost, your brain is providing them back for you. Are the dreams troubling you? Would you call them nightmares?"

Monica thinks about how she feels when she wakes up from the dreams. She's curious about what she dreamed and how it relates to Gran but she's never concerned or scared. Nothing in the dreams has been something she is afraid of. She's not worried about getting sleep. She actually sort of enjoys the connection she's been feeling to Gran thanks to the dreams. "No, not at all. I quite like them, I think," she answers.

"Perfect. So, in my opinion, we wouldn't need to look for a solution to something that isn't a problem."

"Do you believe that these dreams are really memories?" Monica pushes.

"I told you, I believe that your brain wants you to keep these memories alive. Whether they are one hundred percent accurate or not is irrelevant. Honestly, most memories are not completely accurate themselves, if you think about it. I think you should keep writing them down, as you've been doing, to give your brain the peace of mind it needs to know that they aren't being forgotten. Also, if you have other family members who may have the same fears, I suggest you talk about the memories with them."

Monica can tell she's being dismissed, which makes sense. Somer has taken time out of her day to give her opinion. It's the best Monica could've hoped for. She stands up and offers her hand to the expert. "Thank you so much. I appreciate you taking the time to see me and talk with me."

"Not a problem. I hope it helped."

***

The door to the front entry bangs open against the wall with a loud crashing sound. She almost drops the knife she's holding when she jumps at the sound. "Sorry," a voice calls from the living room. "The wind is blowing really hard and the door got away from me." The voice gets closer as the man makes his way into the kitchen doorway. "I didn't mean to slam it. Hope I didn't startle you too badly."
"I didn't drop the knife and I didn't cut myself so I think we're alright," she says.
"Perfect. How are my favorite people today?"
She looks down at her swollen belly and smiles. "I think we're good. Two out of three of us are definitely hungry though so I need to get this dinner finished up."
"Well, then let me help." He grabs an apron from the side of the refrigerator and slips it over his head. Then he grabs the bowl of meat from the counter. "Am I shaping this into burger patties?" he asks.

***

Monica shakes herself to attention. She's been sitting on the floor outside the convention room, waiting for the ridiculously long lunchtime to come to an end so she can go back into the next session. These conferences always give them a couple of hours for lunch. When you're used to grabbing something at your desk between clients, that's entirely too much time. She hadn't meant to doze off against the wall but she'll take the happy accident. She opens the notes app on her phone and quickly records everything she can remember about the pleasant memory she just dreamt. Her grandparents were truly adorable. Of course, she already witnessed that firsthand when she was growing up and had them both. But she likes seeing that they were already like this so early in their marriage. She likes that her grandfather had his own apron. She likes that he came home and jumped in to help. Traditional gender roles didn't seem to exist in their relationship and Monica loves that.

Her Mom has been coming around to the idea that Monica is dreaming about Gran's life. She liked the explanation from Somer that Monica had seen or encountered this before and was just adapting it. Monica didn't push the idea, she's just happy she can talk about it.

The biggest surprise was Greg. He is completely on board. He said he knew something was up from the moment she knew that plumber's name and he is "here for it". He might be enjoying this more than Monica is.

Both of them now have access to this shared note where they can read about the dreams right after they happen. Monica loves being able to share this with them. In fact, Mom will love this one. She and Gran always got along but she and Grandpa had a special bond. Mom loves it when the memories give her warm feelings about Grandpa.

The door to the conference room opens and the presenter steps into the hallway. "I'll leave this open and you can begin filtering in whenever you're ready," she says. Monica knows that's her signal to get up and get back into her day. She finishes typing the last note and closes the app.

***

She pads across the floor, conscious of not slipping on the tile. She stops in front of a mirror and slowly drags her face up toward it. She stares back at herself, lines and wrinkles where she certainly doesn't remember them being before. The skin looks papery and thin, showing purple lines everywhere. She smiles and leans into the mirror so close she can almost touch it with her nose. "It's all up to you now," she whispers. "Remember it all for me." Then she pulls back far enough that her face is in focus again and winks.

***

Monica opens her eyes and stares at the ceiling of her dark bedroom. That felt different, somehow. She scrambles for her phone beside her. It's just after two in the morning. She thumbs open her notes app and tries to recall the details so she can record them.

*Looked into a mirror so I got to see my/her face, it looked
like Gran now.
Mirror was basic, rectangular, silver-edged. Nothing
fancy.
I could see a little of the room behind her in the mirror's
reflection. Couch, table.*

Monica sucks in a breath as she pictures what she saw. Her thumbs fly faster.

*It looked like the room at the facility! This is new.
Whispered "It's all up to you know. Remember it all for
me."
Winked. Definitely winked.*

What does this mean? She realizes this one seems pretty obvious, on the surface. If she's been dreaming memories, does Gran know she's been doing that? Is Gran communicating with her? Has she been doing that all along?

She sits up, wide awake. This feels like a game-changer. This feels like something she needs to talk to someone about. She almost wants to jump in the car and drive to Gran right now. But, of course, they would never allow her to visit in the middle of the night.

In her hand, the phone starts ringing.

Monica looks down at the screen and,

immediately, she understands. It's like all the dots have come together and she sees the picture she's been drawing since that first dream of the house in Virginia.

She swipes the screen and brings the phone to her ear. "Mom?" she says.

There's a sob from the other end that breaks Monica's heart. "Mom, it's ok. You don't have to say it. I think I already know."

"It's Gran," Mom whispers. Her voice is broken and water-logged.

"I know," Monica says. "Mom, it's going to be ok. We'll get through it. I promise."

Afterword

Thank you so much for spending some time with these short stories. If you enjoyed them, I'd recommend following the blog where I often post short scenes or poems. Or, of course, I have full-length works available.

Details and links at tabathashipleybooks.com

www.ingramcontent.com/pod-product-compliance
Lightning Source LLC
Chambersburg PA
CBHW061524310726
48972CB00008B/2315